TURNING THE EYE

Patricia Grace and the Short Story

Turning the Eye

PATRICIA GRACE AND THE SHORT STORY

Judith Dell Panny

Lincoln University Press
and Daphne Brasell Associates Ltd

First published in 1997
by Lincoln University Press
PO Box 195, Lincoln University
Canterbury, Aotearoa New Zealand

and Daphne Brasell Associates Ltd
PO Box 12-214, Thorndon
Wellington, Aotearoa New Zealand

with Whitireia Publishing
Whitireia Community Polytechnic
Private Bag 50-910, Porirua City
Aotearoa New Zealand

© 1997 Short stories: Patricia Grace
© 1997 Commentary: Judith Dell Panny
© 1997 Edition: Lincoln University Press and Daphne Brasell Associates Ltd

All rights reserved.
No part of this publication may be reproduced, stored in a retrieval system, or transmitted in any other form or by any means, electronic, mechanical, including photocopying, recording or otherwise, without the prior written permission of the copyright holder.

The support of the International Pacific College is gratefully acknowledged.

The stories by Patricia Grace are reproduced in this volume as published previously by Penguin Books (NZ) Limited.

ISBN 0-909049-08-4

Designed by Hamish Thompson, Daphne Brasell Associates Ltd, Wellington
Cover illustration from *Te Aitanga ā Kiwa Series: Travellers 2*, by John Bevan Ford
Edited by Vivienne Stanley, Whitireia Publishing, Porirua City
Māori text edited by Jossie Kaa, Huia Publishers, Wellington
Marketing by Amanda Smith, Whitireia Publishing, Porirua City
Typeset by Chris Judd, Auckland
Editorial supervision by Nicky Page, Daphne Brasell Associates Ltd, Wellington
Printed by Astra DPS, Wellington

10 9 8 7 6 5 4 3 2 1

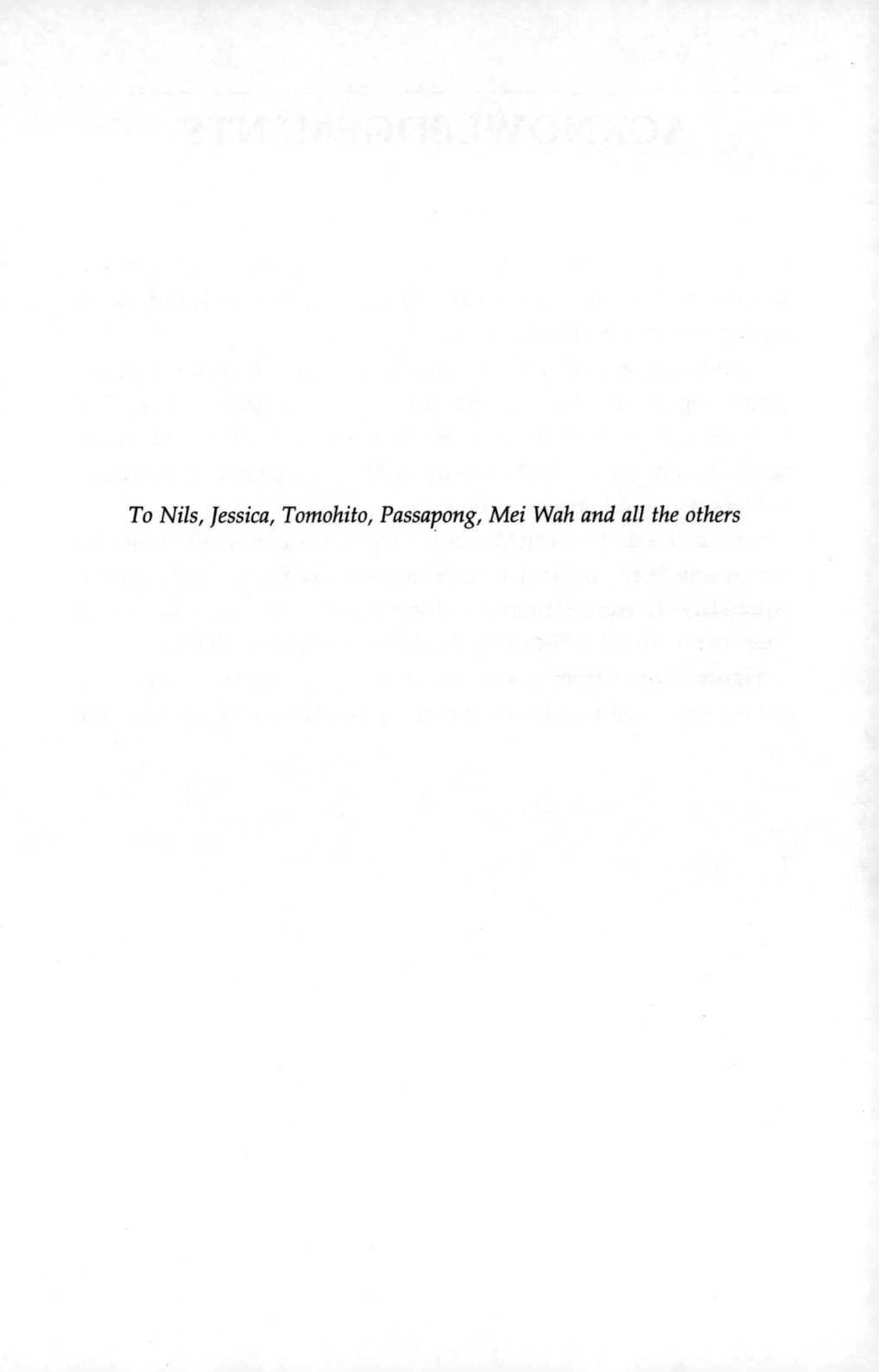

To Nils, Jessica, Tomohito, Passapong, Mei Wah and all the others

ACKNOWLEDGEMENTS

Thanks are due to Patricia Grace for generously allowing the reproduction of these short stories and to Penguin Books NZ Ltd for its approval of this project.

Thanks are also due to International Pacific College (IPC) for supporting this publication and granting me sabbatical leave, thus ensuring that my work would meet the needs and interests of a wide range of students at the University of Trier, the Christian-Albrechts University of Kiel and elsewhere.

Special thanks to Mary McKenzie, IPC's outstanding librarian, for her willing help and to all those involved in the editing process, especially Vivienne Stanley, Andrew Mason and Jossie Kaa (Huia Publishers). To John Bevan Ford, āku mihi ki a koe. Kia ora.

Figure 1 comes from *Tanenuiarangi Booklet* by Paki Harrison (1988), and is reproduced with the permission of The University of Auckland.

CONTENTS

Introduction 1
Patricia Grace 3

1 BETWEEN EARTH AND SKY 7
Text 9
Commentary 13
Glossary and Notes 16

2 VALLEY 17
Text 19
Commentary 42
Glossary and Notes 47

3 JOURNEY 49
Text 51
Commentary 66
Glossary and Notes 70

4 KAHAWAI 73
Text 75
Commentary 80
Glossary and Notes 82

5 OLD ONES BECOME BIRDS 85
Text 87
Commentary 90
Glossary and Notes 94

6 SUN'S MARBLES 97
Text 99
Commentary 104
Glossary and Notes 107

7 **NGATI KANGARU** 109
   Text 111
   Commentary 127
   Glossary and Notes 132

Patricia Grace and the Short Story 139
Overview and Analysis of a Short Story 141
Biographical Outline 143
Publications 144
Bibliography 145

INTRODUCTION

As one of three-and-a-half million New Zealanders, I am astonished at the intense interest of European readers in the work of our writers. Katherine Mansfield and Janet Frame have long been well known and appreciated throughout Germany, Switzerland, Norway, Denmark, Belgium and France. Currently, prose authors creating interest in these countries are Patricia Grace, Witi Ihimaera and Keri Hulme. In Europe today there is a passion for the work of indigenous writers, New Zealand indigenous writers in particular. Students of literature readily state reasons for this: the stories and novels disclose a cultural perspective with something positive to offer, in contrast to some of the disillusioned writing of Western post-modernists. Māori writers embrace and express a value system to which many Europeans respond with enthusiasm.

Appreciation of Māori writing in English is sometimes limited by inadequate knowledge of the Māori and their traditions. Readers can miss the full range of cultural implications. As well as discussing the literary merit of Patricia Grace's writing, this book explores cultural resonances. Commentaries and questions follow each story, along with explanations of language use for readers from other parts of the world. Having been introduced to seven stories, readers may wish to proceed to the full range of Patricia Grace's writing.

There is widespread demand for the primary texts, together with material providing a greater understanding of the New Zealand idiom and guidance in appreciating the significance of underlying cultural premises. In several European countries, Grace's work is already studied by tertiary students of English. *Turning the Eye* addresses needs which these students have identified.

This book is not simply for those (whether in Europe or in New Zealand) for whom English is not their first language. Readers can compare and contrast their own views of the stories with those proposed here. Furthermore, in appreciating more fully this particular selection of stories, readers may develop greater understanding of the skill and discipline required by the short story as a literary form.

PATRICIA GRACE

Fifty-two stories in four volumes show a remarkable diversity, varying greatly in subject matter, style, characterisation and length. 'I've always wanted to write about a variety of ideas in a variety of ways' (Grace interviewed in McRae 1992, p.292). Grace's stories relate to the experiences of people of all ages: children, grandparents, mothers, uncles and friends. The race of some characters is not mentioned. Some are pākehā (European New Zealanders), but most of Grace's characters are Māori, giving stories warmth, expressiveness and a distinctive sense of humour.

Grace discovered that, 'it was the writing coming from my Māori experiences and feelings that was more important to me because I had more to say and more to aim for. Also there is a greater need for Māori to be writing about Māori things, in order that old stereotypes may be broken down, and in order that a Māori standpoint can be taken' (King 1978, p.80). Grace's stories do, in accordance with her stated intention, reveal 'a legitimate and structured way of life, and a real seriousness and a deep spirituality' (King 1978, p.80).

The collection of stories, *Waiariki*, published in 1975, was the first published volume of fiction by a Māori woman. Although she lived in Wellington as a child and was educated at private Catholic schools and Wellington Teachers' College, Grace made regular family visits throughout her childhood to her father's ancestral land near Plimmerton, an outer suburb of Wellington. Hongoeka Bay and the neighbouring rocky coast became the setting for many of her finest stories and for the novel *Potiki*. This is where she and her husband live today.

Thus two traditions have provided Patricia Grace with a rich heritage. She received a formal education in which the traditions of European literature played a significant part, and, as a member of a Māori community, she listened to the old stories and myths and absorbed the essential concepts that underpin Māori culture. In a 1984 address, at the Teachers' Resource Centre in Christchurch, she stated that, for her, Māori culture was defined by certain values: 'I'm talking about "aroha" (love); "manaakitanga" (hospitality); "whanaungatanga" (relationships in the family); "nga tipuna" (ancestors); "te tangata" (the importance of people); "te whenua" (land); "te moana" (the sea). I'm talking about "te mauri"—the life spirit of every person.' These values are fundamental to all her stories.

Grace is a natural storyteller. She captures the music and spirit of an oral story-telling tradition. Whether her characters become the tellers or whether the author-narrator tells the tale, the narrative skill is equally apparent. The stories read well. To hear the author herself reading them aloud, with her fine use of pause and timing, is to gain a full appreciation of her skill and sense of humour.

Critics have noted the mixture of Māori and European idiom and speech rhythms in Patricia Grace's work. What has been termed inconsistency is an essential part of Grace's characterisation. Many of her characters live in both worlds. Older characters, for whom Māori would be the first language, like the old man in 'Journey', speak English with a distinctive Māori rhythm: 'Funny people these pakehas, had to chop up everything. Couldn't talk to a hill or a tree these people, couldn't give the trees or the hills a name and make them special and leave them. Couldn't go round, only through.' He takes pride in knowing more English words than he actually uses in everyday conversation.

Grace claims to write about the 'ordinary people who hadn't been written about before' (McRae 1992, p.292), showing the resilience of families denied the right to determine the way their land is used. She also shows the strength of families living in traditional closeness to the land. Contemporary problems are reflected in many stories. For instance, workers made redundant must depend on their wits to make a living. These are not stories about those who value possessions, but about those who value people and who have a strong sense of family and community. Their lives, supposedly 'ordinary', are extraordinary.

Grace writes with probing honesty. The characters themselves seek to be honest, like the mother in 'Between Earth and Sky' who does not permit any pretence as she speaks to her newborn son. Grace does not recoil from disclosing shameful or unworthy behaviour: racist remarks, discrimination, brutality and abuse. At the same time, there is much in Grace's work that is dignified and celebratory. Both positive and negative aspects of human interaction find expression in her work.

Not only is her observation of people and the natural world accurate, but Grace works from a thorough knowledge of Māori mythology. This is significant in several of her stories. She has carefully researched the historical events which are so important in 'Ngati Kangaru'.

Ken Arvidson is one critic who insists that Grace's stories and novels are 'political in the way they called Pakeha attitudes and practices into question' (McGregor & Williams 1991, p.119). Grace does not deny the political element, but, where Arvidson suggests that Māori writers have 'moral, political and cultural' aims (McGregor & Williams 1991, p.121), Grace maintains that making a political statement is never as important as showing relationships within families and among friends, or finding out about characters and telling their stories (Tausky 1991, p.93).

This focus ensures that Patricia Grace avoids giving the impression that her stories are vehicles for teaching. At the same time, her stories effectively convey cultural attitudes and Māori traditions, disclose legal anomalies, and raise questions which are, indeed, political.

BETWEEN EARTH AND SKY

From *The Dream Sleepers*, 1980

BETWEEN EARTH AND SKY

I walked out of the house this morning and stretched my arms out wide. Look, I said to myself. Because I was alone except for you. I don't think you heard me.

Look at the sky, I said.

Look at the green earth.

How could it be that I felt so good? So free? So full of the sort of day it was? How?

And at that moment, when I stepped from my house, there was no sound. No sound at all. No bird call, or tractor grind. No fire crackle or twig snap. As though the moment had been held quiet, for me only, as I stepped out into the morning. Why the good feeling, with a lightness in me causing my arms to stretch out and out? How blue, how green, I said into the quiet of the moment. But why, with the sharp nick of bone deep in my back and the band of flesh tightening across my belly?

All alone. Julie and Tamati behind me in the house, asleep, and the others over at the swamp catching eels. Riki two paddocks away cutting up a tree he'd felled last autumn.

I started over the paddocks towards him then, slowly, on these heavy knotted legs. Hugely across the paddocks I went almost singing. Not singing because of needing every breath, but with the feeling of singing. Why, with the deep twist and pull far down in my back and cramping between the legs? Why the feeling of singing?

How strong and well he looked. How alive and strong, stooping over the trunk steadying the saw. I'd hated him for days, and now suddenly I loved him again but didn't know why. The saw cracked through the tree setting little splinters of warm wood hopping. Balls of mauve smoke lifted into the air. When he looked up I put my hands to my back and saw him understand me over the skirl of the saw. He switched off, the sound fluttered away.

I'll get them, he said.

We could see them from there, leaning into the swamp, feeling for eel holes. Three long whistles and they looked up and started towards us, wondering why, walking reluctantly.

Mummy's going, he said.

We nearly got one, Turei said. Ay Jimmy, ay Patsy, ay Reuben?

Yes, they said.

Where? said Danny.

I began to tell him again, but he skipped away after the others. It was good to watch them running and shouting through the grass. Yesterday their activity and noise had angered me, but today I was happy to see them leaping and shouting through the long grass with the swamp mud drying and caking on their legs and arms.

Let Dad get it out, Reuben turned, was calling. He can get the lambs out. Bang! Ay Mum, ay?

Julie and Tamati had woken. They were coming to meet us, dragging a rug.

Not you again, they said taking my bag from his hand.

Not you two again, I said. Rawhiti and Jones.

Don't you have it at two o'clock.

We go off at two.

Your boyfriends can wait.

Our sleep can't.

I put my cheek to his and felt his arm about my shoulders.

Look after my wife, he was grinning at them.

Course, what else.

Go on. Get home and milk your cows, next time you see her she'll be in two pieces.

I kissed all the faces poking from the car windows then stood back on the step waving. Waving till they'd gone. Then turning felt the rush of water.

Quick, I said. The water.

Water my foot; that's piddle.

What you want to piddle in our neat corridor for? Sit down. Have a ride.

Helped into a wheelchair and away, careering over the brown lino.

Stop. I'll be good. Stop I'll tell Sister.

Sister's busy.

No wonder you two are getting smart. Stop . . . .

That's it missus, you'll be back in your bikini by summer. Dr McIndoe.

And we'll go water-skiing together. Me.

Right you are. Well, see you both in the morning.

The doors bump and swing.

Sister follows.

Finish off girls. Maitland'll be over soon.

All right Sister.

Yes Sister. Reverently.

The doors bump and swing.

You are at the end of the table, wet and grey. Blood stains your pulsing head. Your arms flail in these new dimensions and your mouth is a circle that opens and closes as you scream for air. All head and shoulders and wide mouth screaming. They have clamped the few inches of cord which is all that is left of your old life now. They draw mucous and bathe your head.

Leave it alone and give it here, I say.

What for? Haven't you got enough kids already?

Course. Doesn't mean you can boss that one around.

We should let you clean your own kid up?

Think she'd be pleased after that neat ride we gave her. Look at the little hoha. God he can scream.

They wrap you in linen and put you here with me.

Well anyway, here you are. He's all fixed, you're all done. We'll blow. And we'll get them to bring you a cuppa. Be good.

The doors swing open.

She's ready for a cuppa Freeman.

The doors bump shut.

Now. You and I. I'll tell you. I went out this morning. Look, I said, but didn't know why. Why the good feeling. Why, with the nick and press of bone deep inside. But now I know. Now I'll tell you and I don't think you'll mind. It wasn't the thought of knowing you, and having you here close to me that gave me this glad feeling, that made me look upwards and all about as I stepped out this morning. The gladness was because at last I was to be free. Free from that great hump that was you, free from the aching limbs and swelling that was you. That was why this morning each stretching of flesh made me glad.

And freedom from the envy I'd felt, watching him these past days, stepping over the paddocks whole and strong. Unable to match his step. Envying his bright striding. But I could love him again this morning.

These were the reasons each gnarling of flesh made me glad as I came out into that cradled moment. Look at the sky, look at the earth, I said. See how blue, how green. But I gave no thought to you.

And now. You sleep. How quickly you have learned this quiet and rhythmic breathing. Soon they'll come and put a cup in my hand and take you away.

You sleep, and I too am tired, after our work. We worked hard you and I and now we'll sleep. Be close. We'll sleep a little while ay, you and I.

COMMENTARY

From the outset, this story is celebratory in tone: 'How was it that I felt so good? So free? So full of the sort of day it was? How?' These questions engage and involve the reader. But another question is even more intriguing. To whom is the first person narrator speaking, since she addresses both herself and 'you'? 'Look, I said to myself. Because I was alone except for you.' She is uncertain as to whether her remarks will be heard.

The answer to the riddle begins to emerge as the narrator describes her physical condition, her slow movement on 'heavy knotted legs' and the 'deep twist and pull far down in my back . . .' It becomes clear that she is due to give birth.

'Between Earth and Sky' is divided into three sections: the opening and concluding sections being joyous and thoughtful in tone; while the middle section, chiefly dialogue, provides light relief through a series of joking remarks between the narrator and the hospital staff. There is at all times a sense of urgency, providing a high level of interest. There is an ever-present impetus or momentum beneath the delight in the blue and green morning, the children playing together, the farewells and the teasing exchanges. But there is none of the anxiety or panic that often attends stories about childbirth.

The title 'Between Earth and Sky' calls to mind the first parents in Māori mythology, Ranginui, the Sky Father, and Papatūānuku, the Earth Mother. The earth and the sky are celebrated in the opening lines and in the concluding paragraphs: 'How blue, how green, I said into the quiet of the moment.' At one level, the narrator can be identified with the Earth Mother, while Riki, her husband, who is sending up clouds of mauve smoke from his power saw, is associated with Rangi watching from a distance between the clouds.

On another level, the mother is one of the children of the earth, who will soon be free again in the light and space between Rangi and Papatūānuku. Riki wields a chain saw, an image of male power.

Though this is a story of family unity rather than male dominance, one is reminded that the woman, burdened with her eighth pregnancy, had 'hated him for days.'

In the traditional Māori world, men and women have spheres of responsibility for which they receive full credit and respect. The day of the child's birth is very special for the mother; it was 'as though the moment had been held quiet, for me only, as I stepped out into the morning.' A new life, and a new era in which she can love her husband again, is about to begin.

Family harmony in this story is established in a few words in the opening scene. Riki perceives his wife's situation at a glance. The children playing at a little distance come directly in response to their father's three long whistles.

Make Lists

1 Which words, phrases, sentences show the children to be spontaneous and secure?

2 Which actions and images contribute to an impression of family harmony in the course of the story?

The mother is confident and forthright, joking with the doctor and cheerfully chiding the nurses. She is quite undaunted when they say, 'Not you again' and when they tease her later:

> Leave it alone and give it here, I say.
> What for? Haven't you got enough kids already?
> Course. Doesn't mean you can boss that one around.

The mother is impatient to hold her new baby and to speak to him. When they are alone, she addresses him seriously, answering thoughtfully the questions posed at the story's opening. The baby is regarded as an individual and as a partner; he and his mother have worked together to achieve the birth. There is no suggestion that this child is less welcome than his brothers and sisters, all of whom have been mentioned by name in the story.

The mother speaks of the 'thought of knowing you'. Māori regard children as the gift of the ancestors, endowed by their ancestors with a unique character and personality. That character is, therefore, respected.

Discussion Topics

Think about the attitudes or beliefs relating to the formation of character and personality that you have encountered.

1 A western view, not universally held but not unfamiliar, is that children should be socialised into a pattern or shape prescribed by their parents. In your opinion, how important is the role of parents in shaping character and personality? Who else could be important in the shaping process?

2 To what extent do you think character and personality are inherited?

The story unfolds in a series of contrasts: earth and sky; joy and physical discomfort; the vigorous man and the burdened woman; hate and love; humour and seriousness; the divine and the familiar. These opposites help to universalise the story, suggesting the complexity attending the birth of a new human being and the complexity of relationships between husband and wife and among family members. This story celebrates an event which is natural and, at the same time, of unparalleled importance and mystery. The reference to earth and sky serves to add significance both to the parents of the child and to the new child; all are the children of the first parents, Papatūānuku and Ranginui.

Overview

The story is the mother's account of the day of the child's birth. Both past and present tenses are used. Explain the reasons for the variation and, in particular, the effect of the use of the present tense.

GLOSSARY AND NOTES

ay	affirmative sound, since 'ae', which has a similar sound, means 'yes' in Māori
careering	travelling at speed
cord	umbilical cord
cradled moment	precious, complete, memorable moment
a cuppa	a cup of tea
eel	long snake-like fish
gnarling	painful twisting and tightening
heavy knotted legs	the legs of a woman pregnant with her eighth child. Irregular lumps would be caused by varicose veins and the heaviness by fluid retention
hōhā (M)	nuisance
hump	heavy bulge
neat	good, exciting, splendid
Papatūānuku (M)	the Earth Mother, in Māori mythology
piddle	urine
Ranginui (M)	the Sky Father, in Māori mythology
Rawhiti and Jones	the surnames of the nurses on duty
skirl of the saw	whirr and whine of the saw
the water	amniotic fluid

VALLEY

From *Waiariki*, 1975

VALLEY

SUMMER

The sun-filled sky wraps the morning in warmth. Already the asphalt has begun to shimmer with light and heat, and the children are arriving.

They spill out of the first bus with sandwiches and cordial, in twos and threes, heads together, strangely quiet. Uncertain they stand with bare feet warming on asphalt, clutching belongings, wondering. They are wondering what I will be like.

It is half past eight. I am watching from my kitchen window and see them glance this way, wondering. In a minute or two I will be ready to go over for them to look at me, but now they are moving away slowly, slapping feet on the warmed playground.

They are wondering what he will be like too. He is in his classroom already, sorting out names, chalking up reminders, and cleaning dead starlings from the grate of the chipheater in the corner. They stand back from the glass doors and stare, and he comes out with the dead birds on a shovel and gives them to a big boy to take away and bury. They all stare, and the younger ones wonder if he killed the birds, but the older ones know that starlings get trapped in the chimneys every summer and have to be cleaned out always on the first day of school.

I pick up the baby and my bag and walk across. Their eyes are on me.

'Hullo,' I say, but no one speaks, and they hurry away to the middle room, which is Tahi's, because they know her. Some of them call her Mrs Kaa because they have been told to; others call her Auntie because she is their aunt; and others call her Hey Tahi because they are little and don't know so much.

At nine he rings the bell and makes a come-here sign with his arm. They see, and know what he wants, and walk slowly to stand on the square of concrete by the staffroom steps. They stand close together, touching, and he tells them his name and mine. Then he reads their names from a list and Tahi tells each where to stand. Soon we have three groups: one for the little room which is mine, one for the middle room which is hers, and one for the big room which is his.

We find a place for the sandwiches and cordial and then they sit looking at me and not speaking, wondering what I am like.

I put the baby on a rug with his toys. I put my bag by the table, then write my name on the board to show them how it looks. And I read it for them so they will know its sound. I write baby's name as well and read it too, but they remain silent.

And when I say good morning they look at one another and at the floor, so I tell them what to say. But, although some open their mouths and show a certain willingness, no sound comes out. Some of them are new and haven't been to school before and all of them are shy.

The silence frightens me, beating strongly into the room like sun through glass.

But suddenly one of them speaks.

He jumps up and points excitedly. Necks swivel.

'Hey ! You fullas little brother, he done a mimi. Na !'

And there is little Eru with a puddle at his feet. And there we are, they and I, with a sentence hanging in the sun-filled room waiting for another to dovetail its ending.

I thank him and ask his name but his mouth is shut again. The little girl in shirt and rompers says, 'He's Samuel.'

'Mop?' Samuel asks, and means shall I get the wet mop from the broom cupboard and clean up the puddle. Which is friendly of him.

'Yes please,' I say, but again he stands confused.

Shirt and rompers shoves him towards the door. 'Go,' she says.

He mops up the water and washes the mop at the outside tap. Then he stands on the soggy mop-strings with his warmed feet, and the water squeezes out and runs in little rivers, then steams dry. Samuel wears large serge shorts belted with a man's necktie and there is one button on his shirt. His large dark eyes bulge from a wide flat face like two spuds. His head is flat too, and his hair has been clipped round in a straight line above his ears. The hair that is left sticks straight up as though he is wearing a kina.

Shirt and rompers tells me all the names and I write them on the board. Her name is Margaret.

Samuel
Margaret
Kopu, Hiriwa
Cowboy
Lillian, Roimata
Glen
Wiki, Steven
Marama, Evelyn
Michael, Edie
Hippy
Stan.

We have made a poem. The last two are twins; I don't know how I'll ever tell them apart.

We find a place for everyone at the tables and a locker for each one's belongings, but although they talk in whispers and nudge one another they do not offer me any words. And when I speak to them they nod or shake their heads. Their eyes take the floor.

The play bell rings and I let them go. They eat briefly, swig at the cordial or go to the drinking taps. Then they pad across the hot asphalt to the big field where the grass is long and dry. Then they begin to run and shout through the long grass as though suddenly they have been given legs and arms, as though the voices have at that moment been put into them.

Ahead of them the grasshoppers flick up and out into the ever-heating day.

Hiriwa sits every morning at the clay table modelling clay. He is a small boy with a thin face and the fingers that press into the clay are long, and careful about what they do.

This morning he makes a cricket—female by the pointed egg-laying mechanism on its tail. He has managed the correct angles of the sets of legs, and shows the fine rasps on the hind set by lifting little specks of clay with his pencil. Soon he will tell me a story so I can write for him; then later he will show the children what he has made and read the story for them.

We collected the crickets yesterday because we are learning about insects and small animals in summer. The crickets are housed in a large jar containing damp earth and stones and a wine biscuit. The book tells me that this is the way to keep crickets, and they seem content enough to live like this as they begin their ringing in the warmth of mid-morning.

Two weeks ago we walked down past the incinerator to where nasturtiums flood a hollow of ground at the edge of bush, covering long grass and fern beginnings with round dollar leaves and orange and gold honey flowers blowing trumpets at the sky.

The first thing was to sit among the leaves and suck nectar from the flowers, which wasn't why we had come but had to be done first. And it gave us a poem for the poem book too. Roimata, who finds a secret language inside herself, gave us the poem:

> I squeeze the tail off the nasturtium flower
> And suck the honey,
> The honey runs all round inside me,
> Making me sweet
> Like sugar,

And treacle,
And lollies,
And chocolate fish.
And all the children lick my skin
And say, 'Sweet, sweet,
Roimata is a sweet, sweet girl.'

The next thing was to turn each flat nasturtium leaf carefully and look on the soft green underside for the pin prick sized butterfly eggs. We found them there, little ovals of yellow, like tiny turned-on light bulbs, and found the mint-green caterpillars too, chewing holes in their umbrellas.

The next thing was to put down the leaves they had picked and to begin rolling down the bank in the long grass, laughing and shouting, which wasn't why we had come but had to be done as well:

I rolled busting down the bank
On cold seagrass,
And I thought I was a wave of the sea,
But I am only a skinny girl
With sticking out eyes,
And two pigtails
That my Nanny plaits every morning
With spider fingers.

Now all the eggs have hatched, and every afternoon they pick fresh leaves for the caterpillars. Every morning we find the leaves eaten to the stems, and the table and floor littered with black droppings like scattered crumbs of burnt toast.

The caterpillars are at several stages of growth. Some are little threads of green cotton, and difficult to see, camouflaged by the leaf and its markings. Others are half grown and working at the business of growing by eating steadily all day and night. The largest ones are becoming sluggish with growth, and have gone away from food and attached themselves to the back of the room to pupate:

The caterpillar,
Up on the classroom wall,
Spins a magic house around itself
To hide from all the boys and girls.

Then yesterday on coming in from lunch we found the first of the butterflies, wing-beating the sun-filled room in convoy. We kept them for the afternoon, then let them out the window and watched them fly away:

Butterfly out in the sun,
Flying high by the roof,
'Look up there,' Kopu said.
'Butterfly. Na.
The best butterfly.
I want to be a butterfly flying.'

I said that he would tell me a story to write about his cricket. And that later he would show the children what he had made and read the story for them. But I turned and saw his arm raised and his fist clenched. His thin arm, with the small fingers curled, like a daisy stem with its flower closed after sundown. The fist came down three times on the carefully modelled insect. Head, thorax, abdomen. He looked at what he'd done and walked away.

'Why?' I asked but he had no words for me.

'That's why, he don't like it,' Samuel told me.

'That's why, his cricket is too dumb,' Kopu said.

Those two have made a bird's nest out of clay and are filling it with little round eggs, heaping the eggs up as high as they will go.

'I made a nest.'

'I made some eggs.'

I made a cricket as best I could with my careful fingers. Then my flower hand thumped three times down on the cricket. Abdomen, thorax, head. And my cricket is nothing but clay.

AUTUMN

Autumn bends the lights of summer and spreads evening skies with reds and golds. These colours are taken up by falling leaves which jiggle at the fingertips of small-handed winds.

Trees give off crowds of starlings which shoot the valley with scarcely a wing beat, flocking together to replace warmth stolen by diminishing sun.

Feet that were soft and supple in summer are hardening now and, although it is warm yet, cardigans and jerseys are turning up in the lost-property box. And John, our neighbour, looks into his vat one morning and sees a single sheet of milk lining the bottom. He puts his herd out and goes on holiday.

Each day we have been visiting the trees—the silver poplar, the liquid amber, and the plum, peach, and apple. And, on looking up through the branches, each day a greater patch of sky is visible. Yet, despite this preoccupation with leaves and colours and change, the greater part of what we see has not changed at all. The gum tree as ever leaves its shed bark, shed twigs, shed branches untidily on its floor, and the pohutukawa remains dull and lifeless after its December spree and has nothing new for this season.

About us are the same green paddocks where cows undulate, rosetting the grass with soft pancake plops; and further on in the valley the variegated greens of the bush begin, then give way to the black-green of distant hills.

They have all gone home. I tidy my table, which is really a dumping ground for insects in matchboxes, leftover lunches and lost property. Then I go out to look for Eru. The boys are pushing him round in the wood cart and he is grinning at the sky with his four teeth, two top and two bottom, biting against each other in ecstasy.

Tahi is in the staffroom peeling an apple. She points the knife into the dimple of apple where the stem is and works the knife carefully in a circle. A thin wisp of skin curls out from the blade. She peels slowly round and down the apple, keeping the skin paper-thin so that there is neither a speck of skin on the apple nor a speck of apple flesh left on the skin. Nor is there a ridge or a bump on the fruit when she has finished peeling. A perfect apple. Skinless. As though it has grown that way on the tree.

Then she stands the apple on a plate and slashes it down the middle with a knife as though it is nothing special and gives me half.

'Gala Day in five days' time,' she says.

'Yes,' I say. 'They'll want to practise for the races.'

'We always have a three-legged and a sack.'

Then Ed comes in and picks up the phone.

'I've got to order a whole lot of stuff for the gala. Gala in five days' time.'

We wake this morning to the scented burning of manuka and, looking out, see the bell-shaped figure of Turei Mathews outlined by the fire's light against the half-lit morning. He stands with his feet apart and his hands bunched on his spread waist, so that his elbows jut. With his small head and his short legs, he looks like a pear man in a fruit advertisement, except that he has a woman's sunhat pulled down over his ears.

Beside him Ron and Skippy Anderson are tossing branches into the flames and turning the burning sticks with shovels. We hear the snap, snap of burning tea tree and see the flames spread and diminish, spread, diminish—watch the ash-flakes spill upwards and outwards into lighting day.

Yesterday afternoon Turei, Ron, and Skippy brought the truckload of wood and the hangi stones and collected the two wire baskets from the hall. They spat on their hands, took up the shovels, and dug the hole, then threw their tools on the back of the truck and went.

Yesterday Ed and the boys put up the tents, moved tables and chairs, and set up trestles. The girls tidied the grounds, covered tables with newspaper, and wrote numbers in books for raffles.

We were worried by clouds yesterday. But now on waking we watch the day lighting clear; we pack our cakes and pickles into a carton and are ready to leave.

By eight o'clock the cars and trucks are arriving and heaving out of their doors bags of corn, kumara, potatoes, pumpkin, and hunks of meat. Women establish themselves under the gum tree with buckets of water, peelers, and vegetable knives. Turei and his helpers begin zipping their knives up and down steel in preparation for slicing into the pork. Tahi is organising the cakes and pickles and other goods for sale, Eru is riding in the wood cart, and Ed is giving out tins for raffle money. I take up my peeler and go towards the gum tree.

Roimata's grandmother is there.

'It's a good day,' she says.

'Yes,' I say. 'We are lucky.'

'I open these eyes this morning and I say to my mokopuna, "The day it is good." She flies all around tidying her room, making her bed, no trouble. Every smile she has is on her face. I look at her and I say, "We got the sun outside in the sky, and we got the sun inside dancing around." I try to do her hair for her. "Hurry, Nanny, hurry," she says. "Anyhow will do." "Anyhow? Anyhow?" I say. "Be patient, Roimata, or they all think it's Turei's dog coming to the gala." '

Opposite me Taupeke smokes a skinny fag, and every now and again takes time off from peeling for a session of coughing. Her face is as old as the hills, but her eyes are young and birdlike and watchful. Her coughing has all the sounds of a stone quarry in full swing, and almost sends her toppling from the small primer chair on which she sits.

'Too much this,' she explains to me, pointing to her tobacco tin. 'Too much cigarette, too much cough.'

And Connie next to her says, 'Yes, Auntie. You take off into space one of these days with your cough.'

She nods. 'Old Taupeke be a sputnik then. Never mind. I take my old tin with me. No trouble.'

Hiriwa's mother is there too. She is pale and serious-looking and very young. Every now and again Hiriwa comes and stands beside her and watches her working; his small hands rest lightly on her arm, his wrist bones protrude like two white marbles. I notice a white scar curving from her temple to her chin.

Tahi comes over and says, 'Right give us a spud,' then spreads her bulk on a primer chair and begins her reverent peeling. A tissue-thin paring spirals downward from her knife.

'How are you Auntie? How are you Connie? How are you Rita? Gee Elsie you want to put your peel in the hangi and throw your kumara away.'

'Never mind,' says Elsie. 'That's the quick way. Leave plenty on for the pigs.'

'Hullo Auntie, hullo ladies. How are all these potato and kumara getting on?' asks Turei. He takes off his sunhat and wipes the sweat from his neck and head.

'Never mind our potato and kumara,' Tahi says. 'What about your stones? Have you cooks got the stones hot? We don't want our pork jumping off our plates and taking off for the hills.'

'No trouble,' Turei says. 'The meal will be superb. Extra delicious.'

'Wii! Listen to him talk.'

'You got a mouthful there Turei!'

'Plenty of kai in the head, that's why,' he says.

'And plenty in the puku too. Na. Plenty of hinu there Turei.'

'Ah well. I'm going. You women slinging off at my figure I better go.'

He puts his hat on and pats his paunch. 'Hurry up with those vegies. Not too much of the yakkety-yak.' He ambles away followed by a bunch of kids and a large scruffy dog.

The sacks are empty. We have peeled the kumara and potatoes, stripped and washed the corn, and cut and skinned the pumpkin. The prepared vegetables are in buckets of water and we stand to go and wash our hands.

But suddenly we are showered with water. We are ankle deep in water and potatoes, kumara, pumpkin, and corn. Connie, who hasn't yet stood, has a red bucket upside down on her lap and she is decorated with peelings. Turei's dog is running round and round and looks as though he has been caught in a storm.

'Turei, look what your mutt did,' Tahi yells, and Turei hurries over to look, while the rest of us stand speechless. Taupeke's cigarette is hanging down her chin like an anaemic worm.

'That mutt of mine, he can't wait for hangi. He has to come and get it now. Hey you kids. Come and pick up all this. Come on you kids.'

The kids like Turei and they hang around. They enjoy watching him get the hangi ready and listening to him talk.

'They're the best stones,' he tells them. 'These old ones that have been used before. From the river these stones.'

The boys take their shirts off because Turei wears only a singlet over his big drum chest.

'How's that, Turei?' they ask, showing off their arm muscles.

'What's that?' he says.

'What you think?'

'I seen pipis in the sand bigger than that.

'You got too much muscles, Turei.'

'Show us, Turei.'

'Better not. Might be you'll get your eyes sore.'

'Go on,' they shout.

So he puts the shovel down, and they all watch the big fist shut and the thick forearm pull up while the great pumpkin swells and shivers at the top of his arm.

'Wii na Turei ! Some more, Turei.'

'You kids don't want any kai? You want full eyes and empty pukus?'

'Some more, Turei. Some more.'

But Turei is shovelling the white-hot stones into the hangi hole. 'You kids better move. Might be I'll get you on the end of this shovel and stick you all in the hole.'

He makes towards them and they scatter.

The prepared food is covered with cloths and the baskets are lowered over the stones. Steam rises as the men turn on the hose. They begin shovelling earth on to the covered food.

'Ready by twelve,' one of them says.

'Better be sweet.'

'Superb. Extra delicious.'

'Na. Listen to the cook talk.'

Over at the chopping arena the men finish setting up the blocks and get ready to stand to. The crowd moves there to watch as the names and handicaps are called. Hiriwa stands opposite his father's block watching.

Different, the father. Unsmiling. Heavy in build and mood. Blunt fingered hands gripping the slim handled axe.

Hiriwa watches for a while, then walks away.

The choppers stand to and the starter calls 'Go' and begins the count. The lowest handicapped hit into their blocks and as the count rises the other axemen join in. The morning is filled with sound as voices rise, as axes strike and wood splits. White chips fly.

By three o'clock the stalls have done their selling. The last bottle of drink has been sold, many of the smaller children are asleep in the cars and trucks, and the older ones have gone down to the big field to play. Some of the tents are down already and the remains of the hangi have been cleared away. At the chopping arena the men are wrenching off the bottom halves of the blocks from the final chop and throwing split wood and chips on to the trucks.

Turei's dog is asleep under a tree. Finally the raffles are drawn.

Joe Blow wins a bag of kumara which he gives to Ed. Ed wins a carton of cigarettes which he gives to Taupeke. And Tahi wins a live sheep, which she tries to put into the boot of her car but which finds its feet and runs out the gate and down the road, chased by all the kids and Turei's dog.

The kids come back and later the dog, but the sheep is never seen again.

> I said to Nanny,
> 'Do my hair anyhow,
> Anyhow,
> Anyhow,
> Today the gala is on.'
> But she said, 'Be patient, Roimata,
> They'll think it's Turei's dog.'

WINTER

> It rains.
> The skies weep.
> As do we.

Earth stands open to receive her and beside the opened earth we stand to give her our farewell.

'Our Auntie, she fell down.' They stood by the glass doors touching each other, eyes filling. Afraid.

'Our Auntie, she fell.'

And I went with them to the next room and found her lying on the floor, Ed bending over her, and the other children standing, frightened. Not knowing.

'Mrs Kaa, she has fallen on the floor.'

Rain.

It has rained for a fortnight, the water topped the river banks then flowed over. The flats are flooded. Water stirred itself into soil and formed a dark oozing mud causing bare feet to become chapped and sore and hard.

> 'Like sky people crying,
> Because the sun is too lazy
> And won't get up,
> And won't shine,
> He is too lazy.
> I shout and shout,
> "Get up, get up you lazy,
> You make the sky people cry,"
> But the sun is fast asleep.'

The trees we have visited daily are bare now, clawing grey fingered at cold winds. Birds have left the trees and gone elsewhere to find shelter, and the insects that in other seasons walk the trunks and branches and hurry about root formations, have tucked themselves into split bark and wood-holes to winter over.

Birds have come closer to the buildings, crowding under ledges and spoutings. We have erected a bird table and every morning put out crumbs of bread, wheat, bacon rind, honey, apple cores, and lumps of fat. And every day the birds come in their winter feathers, pecking at crumbs, haggling over fruit, fat, and honey. Moving from table to ground to rooftop, then back to table.

On John's paddock the pied stilts have arrived, also in search of food, standing on frail red legs, their long thin beaks like straws, dipping into the swampy ground.

'Our Auntie she has fallen.'

I took them out on to the verandah where they stood back out of the rain, looking at the ground, not speaking. I went to the phone. Disbelief as I went to the phone.

An emptiness and an unbelieving.

Because they had all been singing an hour before, and she had been strumming the guitar. And now there was a half sentence printed on the board with a long chalk mark trailing, and a smashed stick of chalk on the floor beside her.

Because at morning break she'd made the tea and he'd said, 'Where's the chocolate cake?' Joking.

'I'll run one up tonight,' she'd said. 'But you'll have to chase the hens around and get me a couple of eggs. My old chooks have gone off the lay.'

'Never mind the eggs,' he'd said. 'Substitute something, like water.'

'Water?' It had put a grin on her face.

'Water?' It had brought a laugh from deep inside her and soon she'd had the little room rocking with sound, which is a way of hers.

Or was. But she lay silent on the schoolroom floor and he came out and spoke to them.

'Mrs Kaa is very sick. Soon the bus will come to take you home. Don't be frightened.' And there was nothing else he could say.

'Our Auntie, she fell down.'

Standing by the glass doors, the pot bellied heater in the corner rumbling with burning pine and the room steaming. She had laughed about my washing too, that morning. My classroom with the naps strung across it steaming in the fire's heat.

'I'm coming in for a sauna this afternoon. And a feed. I'm coming in for a feed too.'

Each morning the children have been finding a feast in the split logs that the big boys bring in for the fire. Kopu and Samuel busy themselves with safety pins, digging into the holes in the wood and finding the dormant white larvae of the huhu beetle.

'Us, we like these.'

And they hook the fat concertina grubs out on the pins and put them on the chip heater to cook.

Soon there is a bacon and roasted peanut smell in the room and the others leave what they are doing and go to look. And wait, hoping there will be enough to go round.

Like two figures in the mist they stood by the doors behind the veil of steam, rain beating behind them. Large drops hitting the asphalt, splintering and running together again.

Eyes filling.

'Mrs Kaa, she fell down.'

Gently they lower her into earth's darkness, into the deep earth. Into earth salved by the touch of sky, the benediction of tears. And sad the cries come from those dearest to her. Welling up, filling the void between earth and sky and filling the beings of those who watch and weep.

'Look what your mutt did Turei.'

'We always have a three-legged and a sack.'

'Water?' the room rocking with sound, the bright apple skinless on a plate, smashed chalk beside her on the floor.

'A sauna and a feed.'

'Our Auntie.'

'Mrs Kaa . . . '

It is right that it should rain today, that earth and sky should meet and touch, mingle. That the soil pouring into the opened ground should be newly blessed by sky, and that our tears should mingle with those of sky and then with earth that receives her.

And it is right too that threading through our final song we should hear the sound of children's voices, laughter, a bright guitar strumming.

SPRING

    The children know about spring.
    Grass grows.
    Flowers come up.
    Lambs drop out.
    Cows have big bags swinging.
    And fat tits.
    And new calves.
    Trees have blossoms.

And boy calves go away to the works on the trucks and get their heads chopped off.

The remainder of the pine has been taken back to the shed, and the chips and wood scraps and ash have been cleaned away from the corner. The big boys make bonfires by the incinerator, heaping on them the winter's debris. Old leaves and sticks and strips of bark from under the pohutukawa and gum, dry brown heads of hydrangea, dead wood from plum, peach, and apple.

Pipiwharauroa has arrived.

'Time for planting,' he calls from places high in the trees.

'Take up spade and hoe, turn the soil, it's planting time.'

So we all go out and plant a memorial garden. A garden that when it matures will be full of colour and fragrance.

Children spend many of their out of school hours training and tending pets which they will parade at the pet show on auction day. They rise early each morning to feed their lambs and calves, and after school brush the animals, walk them, and feed them again.

Hippy and Stan have adopted Michael, who hangs between them like an odd looking triplet. The twins have four large eyes the colour of coal, four sets of false eye lashes and no front teeth. They are a noisy pair. Both like to talk at once and shout at each other, neither likes to listen. They send their words at each other across the top of Michael's head and land punches on one another that way too.

Bang !
'Na Hippy.'
Bang !
'Na Stan.'
Bang !
'Serve yourself right Hippy.'
Bang !
'Serve yourself right Stan.'
Bang !
'Sweet ay?'
Bang !
'Sweet ay?'
Until they both cry.

Michael is the opposite in appearance, having two surprised blue eyes high on his face, and no room to put a pin head between one freckle and the next. His long skinny limbs are the colour of boiled snapper and his hair is bright pink. Without his shirt he looks as though the skin on his chest and the skin on his back is being kept apart by mini tent poles. His neck swings side to side as Hippy punches Stan, and Stan punches Hippy. And Michael joins in the chorus. 'Na Hippy! Sweet? Sweet Stan ay? Serve yourself right.' And when they both cry he joins in that as well.

New books have come, vivid with new ink and sweet with the smell of paint and glue and stiff bright paper.

We find a table on which to display the books, and where they can sit and turn the pages and read. Or where I can sit and read for them and talk about all the newly discovered ideas.

'Hundreds of cats, thousands of cats, millions and billions and trillions of cats.'

'Who goes trip trap, trip trap, trip trap over my bridge?'

'Our brother is lost and I am lost too.'

'Run, run, as fast as you can, you can't catch me I'm the gingerbread man?'

Hiriwa makes a gingerbread man with clay, and Kopu and Samuel make one too.

Out of the ovens jump the gingerbread men, outrunning the old woman, the old man, the cat, the bear. 'That's why, the gingerbread man is too fast.' Then is gone in three snaps of the fox's jaws. Snip, Snap, Snap. Which is sad they think.

'Wii, the fox.'

'Us, we don't like the fox.'

'That's why, the fox is too tough.'

'Cunning that fox.'

Then again the closed hand comes down on clay. Snip. Snap. Snap.

He writes in his diary, 'The gingerbread man is lost and I am lost too.' One side of his face is heavy with bruising.

On the day of the pet show and auction his mother says to me, 'We are going away, Hiriwa and I. We need to go, there is nothing left for us to do. By tomorrow we will be gone.' I go into the classroom to get his things together.

The cars and trucks are here again. The children give the pets a drink of water and a last brush. Then they lead the animals in the ring for the judges to look over, discuss, award prizes to. Some of the pets are well behaved and some are not. Patsy's calf has dug its toes in and refuses to budge, and Patsy looks as though she is almost ready to take Kopu's advice. Kopu is standing on the sideline yelling, 'Boot it in the puku Patsy. Boot it in the puku.' And when the judges tell him to go away he looks put out for a moment. But then he sees Samuel and they run off together, hanging on to each other's shirts calling, 'Boot it in the puku. Boot it in the puku,' until they see somebody's goat standing on the bonnet of a truck, and begin rescue operations.

Inside the building, women from W.D.F.F. are judging cakes and sweets and arrangements of flowers. I go and help Connie and the others prepare lunch.

'Pity we can't have another hangi,' Connie says.

'Too bad, no kumara and corn this time of the year,' Elsie says. 'After Christmas, no trouble.'

Joe Blow stands on a box with all the goods about him. He is a tall man with a broad face. He has a mouth like a letter box containing a few stained stumps of teeth which grow out of his gums at several angles. His large nose is round and pitted like a golf ball, and his little eyes are set deep under thick grey eyebrows which are knotted and tangled like escape proof barbed wire. Above his eyebrows is a ribbon width of corrugated brow, and his hair sits close on top of his head like a small, tight-fitting, stocking stitch beanie. His ears are hand sized and bright red.

'What am I bid ladies, gentlemen, for this lovely chocolate cake? Who'll open the bidding?
Made it myself this morning, all the best ingredients.
What do I get, do I hear twenty-five?
Twenty I've got. Thirty I've got.
Forty cents.
Forty-five.
Forty-five. Forty-five. Gone at forty-five to my old pal Charlie, stingy bugger. You'll have to do better than that mates. Put your hands in your pockets now and what do I get for the coffee cake? Made it and iced it myself this morning. Walnuts on top. Thirty.
I have thirty. Thirty-five here.
Forty-five. Advance on forty-five come on all you cockies, take it home for afternoon tea.
Fifty I have, keep it up friends.
Fifty-five. Sixty, now you're talking.
Sixty-five, sixty-five, seventy.
Seventy again. Seventy for the third time. Sold at seventy and an extra bob for the walnuts, Skippy my boy.
Now this kit of potatoes. What am I bid?'
'Do we keep the kit?' someone calls.
'Did I hear fifty? Fifty? Fifty I've got. Any advance on Fifty?

'Do we keep the kit too?'

'Seventy-five I've got. Come on now grew them myself this morning. Make it a dollar. A dollar I've got.'

'What about the kit?'

'One dollar fifty I've got. One seventy-five. Make it two. Two we've got. Two once, two twice, two sold. Sorry about the kit darling we need it for the next lot.' He tips the potatoes into her lap and gives the kit to one of his helpers to refill.

'Two geranium plants for the garden. Two good plants. What do I get? Come on Billy Boy, take them home for the wife. Make her sweet.'

'I already got something for that.'

'That's had it man, say it with flowers.'

'I got much better.'

'Skiting bugger, twenty-five I've got. Thirty I've got. Advance on thirty? Forty. Forty. Forty again. Forty, sold !'

'Now here's one especially for Turei. Filled sponge decorated with peaches and cream. Come on cook, I'll start you off at forty.
Forty cents ladies, gents, and Charlie, from our friend Turei at the back. And forty-five at the front here, come on Turei. Sixty?
Sixty. And seventy up front.
Eighty. Ninety.
One dollar from the district's most outstanding hangi maker and a dollar twenty from the opposition.
One dollar fifty. Two? Two up front. Two fifty from the back.
Two fifty, two fifty . . . Three.
Three we have, come on friend.
Three fifty. What do you say Turei?
Five. Five from the back there.
Five once, five twice, five sold. One cream sponge to Turei the best cook in the district. Thank you boys.

Time's getting on friends. What do you say to a leg a mutton, a bunch a silver beet, a jar a pickle, a bag a spuds, there's your dinner.

VALLEY 39

A dollar? Two? Two ten, twenty, fifty, seventy. Two seventy, two seventy, two seventy, no mucking around, sold.

Another kit of potatoes. I'll take them myself for fifty. Will you let me take them home for fifty? Seventy. Seventy to you, eighty to me. Ninety to you, a dollar to me. Dollar twenty, OK, one fifty. Let me have them for one fifty? One fifty to me, ladies and gents and Charlie. One seventy-five? OK, one ninety. Two?
Two we have once, two we have twice, two for the third time, sold. All yours boy, I've got two acres of my own at home.

Here we are friends, another of these lovely home made sponges. What do you say Turei . . . ?'

But Turei is away under the gum tree sharing his cake with a lot of children and his dog.

And back again to summer, with all the children talking about Christmas and holidays, their pockets bulging with ripe plums.

The branches of the pohutukawa are flagged in brilliant red, and three pairs of tuis have arrived with their odd incongruous talking, 'See-saw, Crack, Burr, Ding. See-saw, See-saw, Ding.' By the time they have been there a week they are almost too heavy to fly, their wings beat desperately in flight in order to keep their heavy bodies airborne.

On the last day of school we wait under the pohutukawa for the bus to arrive, and a light wind sends down a shower of nectar which dries on our arms and legs and faces in small white spots.

They scramble into the bus talking and pushing, licking their skins. They heave their belongings under the seats and turn to the windows to wave. Kopu and Samuel who are last in line stand on the bus step and turn.

'Goodbye,' Kopu says, and cracks Sam in the ribs with his elbow.

'Goodbye,' Samuel says and slams his hands down on top of his kina and blushes.

As the bus pulls away we hear singing. Waving hands protrude from the windows on either side. Hippy, Michael, and Stan have their heads together at the back window, and Roimata is there too, waving, chewing a pigtail—

> 'I am a tui bird,
> Up in the pohutukawa tree,
> And a teacher and some children came out
> And stood under my tree,
> And honey rained all over them,
> But I am a tui bird,
> And when I fly
> It sounds like ripping rags.'

COMMENTARY

'Valley' is set in a country district in any one of New Zealand's valleys. The story is in four sections, encompassing a whole school year.

Summer

There is anxiety among the children as they arrive at school for the start of the new year. A sense of immediacy is created by the use of the present tense.

The point of view moves to the teller of the story, the teacher herself. The narrator and her husband are new teachers in a three-teacher country school. Their toddler accompanies his mother into 'the little classroom' where she will teach the youngest children. At times of teacher shortage in New Zealand and where childcare facilities were unavailable, it was not uncommon for a pre-school child to accompany a teaching mother in the classroom.

It is likely that the teacher is Māori as she understands the Māori words spoken by the children and she compares the hair of one child to a 'kina', Māori for sea-egg. Her baby is named Eru, a Māori name.

The tension of the opening scene increases after the children and teacher enter their classroom. The children are alarmingly silent, until there is a sudden outburst from one of them: ' "Hey you fullas little brother, he done a mimi. Na!" ' In Māori, 'na' adds emphasis. It is often in the sense of 'See!', indicating proof of a statement. The 'mimi' is a puddle of urine made by baby Eru. The speaker, Samuel, is used to the ways of little brothers, but he is not yet aware of the relationship between the two new teachers and the child. 'Fullas' is a Māori adaptation of 'fellows'.

The special appeal of 'Valley' derives, in large measure, from the personal warmth of the narrator, who respects each child and views each one positively: ' "Mop?" Samuel asks, and means shall I get the wet mop from the broom cupboard and clean up the puddle. Which is friendly of him.' During the playtime the teacher shows her interest in the children by observing them:

> they pad across the hot asphalt to the big field where the grass is long and dry. Then they begin to run and shout through the long grass as though suddenly they have been given legs and arms, as though the voices have at that moment been put into them.

The teacher introduces the children to the creatures and the plants they study, draw, write about, mould in clay. The children's poetry, described as 'a secret language', is simple, spontaneous and remarkably effective. Here is an example:

> I rolled busting down the bank
> On cold seagrass,
> And I thought I was a wave of the sea
> But I am only a skinny girl
> With sticking out eyes
> And two pigtails
> That my Nanny plaits every morning
> With spider fingers.

Autumn

It is not only the children's poetry that makes this story poetic. Descriptions of the autumn light, the colours of the leaves and even the feet of the children have the music and accuracy of poetry.

> Autumn bends the lights of summer and spreads evening skies with reds and golds.
> ... And on looking up through the branches, each day a greater patch of sky is visible.
> ... The gum tree as ever leaves its shed bark, shed twigs, shed branches untidily on its floor ...

Autumn's special event is a Gala Day, part of the annual programme of most New Zealand schools. The community comes together to make it a success. In 'Valley', preparation of a hāngi and eating the food cooked in this way is an important part of the day's activites. Cheerful remarks generate a humour among helpers, characteristic of Grace's stories. Turei, who has been preparing the hāngi, is teased by the women. ' "Have you cooks got the stones hot? We don't want our pork jumping off our plates and taking off for the hills." '

Men are responsible for digging a pit for a hāngi and placing large stones on the fire-wood along its base. Wrapped in tin foil and placed in wire baskets, the food is laid on top of the hot stones and covered with cloth and with earth. Uncovered two to three hours later, it should be well cooked with a distinctive flavour and all the juices intact.

Other events characterise gala days everywhere: stalls selling produce and other items which people have donated, raffles, running races for the children and competitions for the adults such as wood-chopping by axemen.

Winter

The winter section begins with a burial. Rain, when a Māori dies is interpreted as the tears of Ranginui, the Sky Father, thus adding mana or prestige to the person who has died. What is remarkable is the sadness and, at the same time, the absence of sentimentality. Patricia Grace achieves this in two ways.

Firstly, the events of the funeral are linked to mythology. The weeping of the people is compared to the weeping by Rangi, the Sky Father, when he and Papatūānuka, the Earth Mother, were separated. The myth provides an objective counterpart or parallel to the grief of the people in the story.

Secondly, a succession of clear and brief images takes the reader from the present moment at the burial back to the fear of the children as they describe what happened to their teacher: ' "Mrs Kaa, she has fallen on the floor." ' The ordinary, cheerful and amusing events from the earlier part of the day—a child's winter poem, images of a winter landscape—follow in rapid succession. The reaction of the children is understated: 'Eyes filling.' Back at the funeral, the coffin is being lowered 'into the deep earth. Into earth salved by the touch of sky . . .' And then, through the mind of the narrator, Mrs Kaa's cheerful words and her laughter are recalled. The section concludes with children singing to a guitar. The focus has moved swiftly back and forth in time, from one impression to another, interspersing cheerful memories with the sadness of the funeral and the shock at Mrs Kaa's collapse.

Spring

This section forms a finale. There is excitement accompanying the arrival of spring, a time of activity and change. There is more fund-raising, this time in the form of an Auction Day. Once again good humour and sharing abound. There are parallels between the behaviour of the community in autumn and in spring, despite the loss sustained in winter. The school year comes to an end. Children leave by bus on the last day of the year, just as they arrived by bus at the opening. A sense of continuity and equilibrium is suggested by the very pattern and shape of the story.

Discussion Topics

1 Can you describe school festivals or gatherings (and the reasons for them) which take place either in New Zealand or in other parts of the world?

2 What might the new teacher have taught the youngest children to value in the course of the year?

3 How has the teacher-narrator fostered enjoyment in learning?

4 Compare the way the children act in the concluding paragraphs with their behaviour at the opening of the story.

Language

It becomes clear that most of the children in the 'Valley' classes come from a Māori community, though this is never stated. Samuel's English is effective in terms of communication, but is not grammatically correct. Like all young children he makes mistakes. Samuel is in a class of new entrants, five- and six-year-olds. But at the same time, the rhythm of the English sentence has been patterned on the rhythm of the Māori sentence. In Māori, one would say, 'Koina, kaore ia e whakaae.' The word 'Koina' would be translated, 'that's why' or 'here's the reason', although Māori has no verb 'to be'. The same structure, beginning, 'That's why', occurs in the sentence, 'That's why, his cricket is too dumb.'

The sentence, ' "Too much cigarette, too much cough" ', reflects a typical Māori language structure in which no verb is necessary. In Māori, the statement would be, 'Ka nui te kaipaipa, ka nui te rewharewha.' 'Ka nui' means 'too much', 'te kaipaipa' means 'cigarettes' collectively and 'te rewharewha' means 'coughing'.

Likewise, in the statement ' "From the river these stones" ', the Māori word order is 'Nō te awa, ēnei kōhatu.' 'Nō te awa' means 'from the river' and 'ēnei kōhatu' means 'these stones'. The sentence, while complete in Māori, is incomplete in English.

In the following, the adjective is the first element in the statement, as is frequently the case in Māori. 'Different the father': 'He rerekē, te matua', and ' "Cunning that fox" ': 'He mūrere, te tauiwi ra.' The same word order is apparent in the speech of the old man in 'Journey': 'Funny people those town people.'

In Māori, tenses are indicated by different introductory particles, whereas in English a change of tense is indicated by adding a suffix, by altering the verbal stem, or by the addition of auxiliaries. Thus, a Māori speaker may sometimes omit a verbal auxiliary that is part of standard English: ' "We got the sun outside in the sky . . ." ' or ' "What you think?" ' or ' "You take off into space one of these days with your cough." '

Patricia Grace captures skilfully the word order and rhythm of speakers of English from Māori communities. The language patterns used by them contribute to the authenticity of the characterisation.

GLOSSARY AND NOTES

chip-heater	an old-fashioned, wood-burning stove; burner for heating water
chooks	hens
cockies	farmers
corn	sweet corn on the cob, different in quality from that fed to animals
fag	cigarette
a feed	a meal
gone off the lay	stopped laying eggs
hāngi (M)	Māori oven in which food is steamed
hinu (M)	fat
huhu (M) beetle	native beetle
hunks	big slabs
kai in the head	literally, 'food in the head'; he means intelligence'
kina (M)	a sea-egg, which is a creature with a spiky outer shell
kit (M)	flax basket
kūmara (M)	sweet potato
mana (M)	integrity, prestige
mokopuna (M)	grandchildren, descendants who are children
mutt	dog
Papatūānuku (M)	the Earth Mother, in Māori mythology
pipi (M)	small shellfish
pīpīwharauroa (M)	shining cuckoo

pohutukawa (M)	native tree bearing red flowers in December
puku (M)	stomach
Ranginui (M)	the Sky Father, in Māori mythology
rompers	baggy shorts with elastic round the legs
run one up	make one quickly
a sack	short for 'a sack race', in which each contestant steps into a sack, holding the top at waist level, and then runs or jumps with leg movement impeded by the sack
serge	a stoutly woven woollen fabric
skiting bugger	boastful person
slinging off	teasing
snapper	sea water fish
spuds	potatoes
tea-tree	manuka (M), native scrub
a three-legged	short for 'a three-legged race', in which contestants run in pairs. Two legs, one from each member of the pair, are tied together
tressles	long make-shift tables with fold-away legs for easy storage
tui (M)	native birds, producing a fine range of sounds. Also known as parson bird because of its tuft of white feathers at the throat
yakkety-yak	talking
you kids	you children
WDFF	Women's Division of Federated Farmers

JOURNEY

From The Dream Sleepers, 1980

JOURNEY

He was an old man going on a journey. But not really so old, only they made him old buttoning up his coat for him and giving him money. Seventy-one that's all. Not a journey, not what you would really call a journey—he had to go in and see those people about his land. Again. But he liked the word Journey even though you didn't quite say it. It wasn't a word for saying only for saving up in your head, and that way you could enjoy it. Even an old man like him, but not what you would call properly old.

The coat was good and warm. It was second-hand from the jumble and it was good and warm. Could have ghosts in it but who cares, warm that's the main thing. If some old pakeha died in it that's too bad because he wasn't scared of the pakeha kehuas anyway. The pakeha kehuas they couldn't do anything, it was only like having a sheet over your head and going woo-oo at someone in the lavatory . . . .

He better go to the lavatory because he didn't trust town lavatories, people spewed there and wrote rude words. Last time he got something stuck on his shoe. Funny people those town people.

Taxi.

It's coming Uncle.

Taxi Uncle. They think he's deaf. And old. Putting more money in his pocket and wishing his coat needed buttoning, telling him it's windy and cold. Never mind, he was off. Off on his journey, he could get round town good on his own good as gold.

Out early today old man.

Business young fulla.

Early bird catches the early worm.

It'll be a sorry worm young fulla, a sorry worm.

Like that is it?

Like that.

You could sit back and enjoy the old taxi smells of split upholstery and cigarette, and of something else that could have been the young fulla's hair oil or his b.o. It was good. Good. Same old taxi same old stinks. Same old shop over there, but he wouldn't be calling in today, no. And tomorrow they'd want to know why. No, today he was going on a journey, which was a good word. Today he was going further afield, and there was a word no one knew he had. A good wind today but he had a warm coat and didn't need anyone fussing.

Same old butcher and same old fruit shop, doing all right these days not like before. Same old Post Office where you went to get your pension money, but he always sent Minnie down to get his because he couldn't stand these old-age people. These old-age people got on his nerves. Yes, same old place, same old shops and roads, and everything cracking up a bit. Same old taxi. Same old young fulla.

How's the wife?

Still growling old man.

What about the kids?

Costing me money.

Send them out to work that's the story.

I think you're right you might have something there old man. Well here we are, early. Still another half hour to wait for the train.

Best to be early. Business.

Guess you're right.

What's the sting?

Ninety-five it is.

Pull out a fistful and give the young fulla full eyes. Get himself out on to the footpath and shove the door, give it a good hard slam. Pick me up later young fulla, ten past five. Might as well make a day of it, look round town and buy a few things.

Don't forget ten past five.

Right you are old man five ten.

People had been peeing in the subway the dirty dogs. In the old days all you needed to do to get on to the station was to step over the train tracks, there weren't any piss holes like this to go through, it wasn't safe. Coming up the steps on to the platform he could feel the quick huffs of his breathing and that annoyed him, he wanted to swipe at the huffs with his hand. Steam engines went out years ago.

Good sight though seeing the big engines come bellowing through the cutting and pull in squealing, everything was covered in soot for miles those days.

New man in the ticket office, looked as though he still had his pyjamas on under his outfit. Miserable looking fulla and not at all impressed by the ten-dollar note handed through to him. A man feels like a screwball yelling through that little hole in the glass and then trying to pick up the change that sourpuss has scattered all over the place. Feels like giving sourpuss the fingers, yes. Yes he knows all about those things, he's not deaf and blind yet, not by a long shot.

Ah warmth. A cold wait on the platform but the carriages had the heaters on, they were warm even though they stank. And he had the front half of the first carriage all to himself. Good idea getting away early. And right up front where you could see everything. Good idea coming on his own, he didn't want anyone fussing round looking after his ticket, seeing if he's warm and saying things twice. Doing his talking for him, made him sick. Made him sick them trying to walk slow so they could keep up with him. Yes he could see everything. Not many fishing boats gone out this morning and the sea's turning over rough and heavy—Tamatea that's why. That's something they don't know all these young people, not even those fishermen walking about on their decks over there. Tamatea a Ngana, Tamatea Aio, Tamatea Whakapau—when you get the winds—but who'd believe you these days. They'd rather stare at their weather on television and talk about a this and a that coming over because there's nothing else to believe in.

Now this strip here, it's not really land at all, it's where we used to get our pipis, any time or tide. But they pushed a hill down over it and shot the railway line across to make more room for cars. The train driver knows it's not really land and he is speeding up over this strip. So fast you wait for the nose dive over the edge into the sea, especially when you're up front like this looking. Well too bad. Not to worry, he's nearly old anyway and just about done his dash, so why to worry if they nose dive over the edge into the sea. Funny people putting their trains across the sea. Funny people making land and putting pictures and stories about it in the papers as though it's something spectacular, it's a word you can use if you get it just right and he could surprise quite a few people if he wanted to. Yet other times they go on as though land is just a nothing. Trouble is he let them do his talking for him. If he'd gone in on his own last time and left those fusspots at home he'd have got somewhere. Wouldn't need to be going in there today to tell them all what's what.

Lost the sea now and coming into a cold crowd. This is where you get swamped, but he didn't mind, it was good to see them all get in out of the wind glad to be warm. Some of his whanaungas lived here but he couldn't see any of them today. Good job too, he didn't want them hanging round wondering where he was off to on his own. Nosing into his business. Some of the old railway houses still there but apart from that everything new, houses, buildings, roads. You'd never know now where the old roads had been, and they'd filled a piece of the harbour up too to make more ground. A short row of sooty houses that got new paint once in a while, a railway shelter, and a lunatic asylum and that was all. Only you didn't call it that these days, he'd think of the right words in a minute.

There now the train was full and he had a couple of kids sitting by him wearing plastic clothes, they were gog-eyed stretching their necks to see. One of them had a snotty nose and a wheeze.

On further it's the same—houses, houses—but people have to have houses. Two or three farms once, on the cold hills, and a rough road going through. By car along the old road you'd always see a pair of them at the end of the drive waving with their hats jammed over their ears. Fat one and a skinny one. Psychiatric hospital, those were the words to use these days, yes don't sound so bad. People had to have houses and the two or three farmers were dead now probably. Maybe didn't live to see it all. Maybe died rich.

The two kids stood swaying as they entered the first tunnel, their eyes stood out watching for the tunnel's mouth, waiting to pass out through the great mouth of the tunnel. And probably the whole of life was like that, sitting in the dark watching and waiting. Sometimes it happened and you came out into the light, but mostly it only happened in tunnels. Like now.

And between the tunnels they were slicing the hills away with big machines. Great-looking hills too and not an easy job cutting them away, it took pakeha determination to do that. Funny people these pakehas, had to chop up everything. Couldn't talk to a hill or a tree these people, couldn't give the trees or the hills a name and make them special and leave them. Couldn't go round, only through. Couldn't give life, only death. But people had to have houses, and ways of getting from one place to another. And anyway who was right up there helping the pakeha to get rid of things—the Maori of course, riding those big machines. Swooping round and back, up and down all over the place. Great tools the Maori man had for his carving these days, tools for his new whakairo, but there you are, a man had to eat. People had to have houses, had to eat, had to get from here to there—anyone knew that. He wished the two kids would stop crackling, their mothers dressed them in rubbish clothes that's why they had colds.

Then the rain'll come and the cuts will bleed for miles and the valleys will drown in blood, but the pakeha will find a way of mopping it all up no trouble. Could find a few bones amongst that lot too. That's what you get when you dig up the ground, bones.

Now the next tunnel, dark again. Had to make sure the windows were all shut up in the old days or you got a face full of soot.

And then coming out of the second tunnel that's when you really had to hold your breath, that's when you really had to hand it to the pakeha, because there was a sight. Buildings miles high, streets and steel and concrete and asphalt settled all round the great-looking curve that was the harbour. Water with ships on it, and roadways threading up and round the hills to layer on layer of houses, even in the highest and steepest places. He was filled with admiration. Filled with Admiration, which was another word he enjoyed even though it wasn't really a word for saying, but yes he was filled right to the top—it made him tired taking it all in. The kids too, they'd stopped crackling and were quite still, their eyes full to exploding.

The snotty one reminded him of George, he had pop eyes and he sat quiet not talking. The door would open slowly and the eyes would come round and he would say I ran away again Uncle. That's all. That's all for a whole week or more until his mother came to get him and take him back. Never spoke, never wanted anything. Today if he had time he would look out for George.

Railway station much the same as ever, same old platforms and not much cleaner than the soot days. Same old stalls and looked like the same people in them. Underground part is new. Same cafeteria, same food most likely, and the spot where they found the murdered man looked no different from any other spot. Always crowded in the old days especially during the hard times. People came there in the hard times to do their starving. They didn't want to drop dead while they were on their own most probably. Rather all starve together.

Same old statue of Kupe with his woman and his priest, and they've got the name of the canoe spelt wrong his old eyes aren't as blind as all that. Same old floor made of little coloured pieces and blocked into patterns with metal strips, he used to like it but now he can just walk on it. Big pillars round the doorway holding everything in place, no doubt about it you had to hand it to the pakeha.

Their family hadn't starved, their old man had seen to that. Their old man had put all the land down in garden, all of it, and in the weekends they took what they didn't use round by horse and cart. Sometimes got paid, sometimes swapped for something, mostly got nothing but why to worry. Yes great looking veges they had those days, turnips as big as pumpkins, cabbages you could hardly carry, big tomatoes, lettuces, potatoes, everything. Even now the ground gave you good things. They had to stay home from school for the planting and picking, usually for the weeding and hoeing as well. Never went to school much those days but why to worry.

Early, but he could take his time, knows his way round this place as good as gold. Yes he's walked all over these places that used to be under the sea and he's ridden all up and down them in trams too. This bit of sea has been land for a long time now. And he's been in all the pubs and been drunk in all of them, he might go to the pub later and spend some of his money. Or he could go to the continuous pictures but he didn't think they had them any more. Still, he might celebrate a little on his own later, he knew his way round this place without anyone interfering. Didn't need anyone doing his talking, and messing things up with all their letters and what not. Pigeons, he didn't like pigeons, they'd learned to behave like people, eat your feet off if you give them half a chance.

And up there past the cenotaph, that's where they'd bulldozed all the bones and put in the new motorway. Resited, he still remembered the newspaper word, all in together. Your leg bone, my arm bone, someone else's bunch of teeth and fingers, someone else's head, funny people. Glad he didn't have any of his whanaungas underground in that place. And they had put all the headstones in a heap somewhere promising to set them all up again *tastefully*—he remembered—didn't matter who was underneath. Bet there weren't any Maoris driving those bulldozers, well why to worry it's not his concern, none of his whanaungas up there anyway.

Good those old trams but he didn't trust these crazy buses, he'd rather walk. Besides he's nice and early and there's nothing wrong with his legs. Yes, he knows this place like his own big toe, and by Jove he's got a few things to say to those people and he wasn't forgetting. He'd tell them, yes.

The railway station was a place for waiting. People waited there in the old days when times were hard, had a free wash and did their starving there. He waited because it was too early to go home, his right foot was sore. And he could watch out for George, the others had often seen George here waiting about. He and George might go and have a cup of tea and some kai.

He agreed. Of course he agreed. People had to have houses. Not only that, people had to have other things—work, and ways of getting from place to place, and comforts. People needed more now than they did in his young days, he understood completely. Sir. Kept calling him Sir, and the way he said it didn't sound so well, but it was difficult to be sure at first. After a while you knew, you couldn't help knowing. He didn't want any kai, he felt sick. His foot hurt.

Station getting crowded and a voice announcing platforms. After all these years he still didn't know where the voice came from but it was the same voice, and anyway the trains could go without him it was too soon. People.

Queuing for tickets and hurrying towards the platforms, or coming this way and disappearing out through the double doors, or into the subway or the lavatory or the cafeteria. He was too tired to go to the lavatory and anyway he didn't like . . . . Some in no hurry at all. Waiting. You'd think it was starvation times. Couldn't see anyone he knew.

I know I know. People have to have houses, I understand and it's what I want.

Well it's not so simple Sir.

It's simple. I can explain. There's only the old place on the land and it needs bringing down now. My brother and sister and I talked about it years back. We wrote letters . . . .

Yes yes but it's not as simple as you think.

But now they're both dead and it's all shared—there are my brother's children, my sister's children, and me. It doesn't matter about me because I'm on the way out, but before I go I want it all done.

As I say it's no easy matter, all considered.

Subdivison. It's what we want.

There'll be no more subdivision Sir, in the area.

Subdivision. My brother has four sons and two daughters, my sister has five sons. Eleven sections so they can build their houses. I want it all seen to before . . . .

You must understand Sir that it's no easy matter, the area has become what we call a development area, and I've explained all this before, there'll be no more subdivision.

Development means houses, and it means other things too, I understand that. But houses, it's what we have in mind.

And even supposing Sir that subdivision were possible, which it isn't, I wonder if you fully comprehend what would be involved in such an undertaking.

I fully comprehend . . . .

Surveying, kerbing and channelling and formation of adequate access, adequate right of ways. The initial outlay . . . .

I've got money, my brother and sister left if for the purpose. And my own, my niece won't use any of my money, it's all there. We've got the money.

However that's another matter, I was merely pointing out that it's not always all plain sailing.

All we want is to get it divided up so they can have a small piece each to build on . . . .

As I say, the area, the whole area, has been set aside for development. All in the future of course but we must look ahead, it is necessary to be far-sighted in these concerns.

Houses, each on a small section of land, it's what my niece was trying to explain . . . .

You see there's more to development than housing. We have to plan for roading and commerce, we have to set aside areas for educational and recreational facilities. We've got to think of industry, transportation . . . .

But still people need houses. My nieces and nephews have waited for years.

They'd be given equivalent land or monetary compensation of course.

But where was the sense in that, there was no equal land. If it's your stamping ground and you have your ties there, then there's no land equal, surely that wasn't hard to understand. More and more people coming in to wait and the plastic kids had arrived. They pulled away from their mother and went for a small run, crackling. He wished he knew their names and hoped they would come and sit down by him, but no, their mother was striding, turning them towards a platform because they were getting a train home. Nothing to say for a week or more and never wanted anything except sitting squeezed beside him in the armchair after tea until he fell asleep. Carry him to bed, get in beside him later then one day his mother would come. It was too early for him to go home even though he needed a pee.

There's no sense in it don't you see? That's their stamping ground and when you've got your ties there's no equal land. It's what my niece and nephew were trying to explain the last time, and in the letters . . . .

Well Sir I shouldn't really do this, but if it will help clarify the position I could show you what has been drawn up. Of course it's all in the future and not really your worry . . . .

Yes yes I'll be dead but that's not . . . .

I'll get the plans.

And it's true he'll be dead, it's true he's getting old, but not true if anyone thinks his eyes have had it because he can see good enough. His eyes are still good enough to look all over the paper and see his land there, and to see that his land has been shaded in and had 'Off Street Parking' printed on it.

He can see good close up and he can see good far off, and that's George over the other side standing with some mates. He can tell George anywhere no matter what sort of get-up he's wearing. George would turn and see him soon.

But you can't, that's only a piece of paper and it can be changed, you can change it. People have to live and to have things. People need houses and shops but that's only paper, it can be changed.

It's all been very carefully mapped out. By experts. Areas have been selected according to suitability and convenience. And the aesthetic aspects have been carefully considered . . . .

Everything grows, turnips the size of pumpkins, cabbages you can hardly carry, potatoes, tomatoes . . . . Back here where you've got your houses, it's all rock, land going to waste there . . . .

You would all receive equivalent sites . . . .

Resited . . . .

As I say on equivalent land . . . .

There's no land equal . . . .

Listen Sir, it's difficult but we've got to have some understanding of things. Don't we?

Yes yes I want you to understand, that's why I came. This here, it's only paper and you can change it. There's room for all the things you've got on your paper, and room for what we want too, we want only what we've got already, it's what we've been trying to say.

Sir we can't always have exactly what we want . . . .

All round here where you've marked residential it's all rock, what's wrong with that for shops and cars. And there'll be people and houses. Some of the people can be us, and some of the houses can be ours.

Sure, sure. But not exactly where you want them. And anyway Sir there's no advantage do you think in you people all living in the same area?

It's what we want, we want nothing more than what is ours already.

It does things to your land value.

He was an old man but he wanted very much to lean over the desk and swing a heavy punch.

No sense being scattered everywhere when what we want . . . .

It immediately brings down the value of your land . . . .

. . . is to stay put on what is left of what has been ours since before we were born. Have a small piece each, a small garden, my brother and sister and I discussed it years ago.

Straight away the value of your land goes right down.

Wanted to swing a heavy punch but he's too old for it. He kicked the desk instead. Hard. And the veneer cracked and splintered. Funny how quiet it had become.

You ought to be run in old man, do you hear.

Cripes look what the old blighter's gone and done. Look at Paul's desk.

He must be whacky.

He can't do that Paul, get the boss along to sort him out.

Get him run in.

Get out old man, do you hear.

Yes he could hear, he wasn't deaf, not by a long shot. A bit of trouble getting his foot back out of the hole, but there, he was going, and not limping either, he'd see about this lot later. Going, not limping, and not going to die either. It looked as though their six eyes might all fall out and roll on the floor.

There's no sense, no sense in anything, but what use telling that to George when George already knew sitting beside him wordless. What use telling George you go empty handed and leave nothing behind, when George had always been empty handed, had never wanted anything except to have nothing.

How are you son?

All right Uncle. Nothing else to say. Only sitting until it was late enough to go.

Going, not limping, and not going to die either.

There you are old man, get your feet in under that heater. Got her all warmed up for you.

Yes young fulla that's the story.

The weather's not so good.

Not the best.

How was your day all told?

All right.

It's all those hard footpaths, and all the walking that gives people sore feet, that's what makes your legs tired.

There's a lot of walking about in that place.

You didn't use the buses?

Never use the buses.

But you got your business done?

All done. Nothing left to do.

That's good then isn't it?

How's your day been young fulla?

A proper circus.

Must be this weather.

It's the weather, always the same in this weather.

This is your last trip for the day is it?

A couple of trains to meet after tea and then I finish.

Home to have a look at the telly.

For a while, but there's an early job in the morning . . . .

Drop me off at the bottom young fulla. I'm in no hurry. Get off home to your wife and kids.

No, no, there's a bad wind out there, we'll get you to your door. Right to your door, you've done your walking for the day. Besides I always enjoy the sight of your garden, you must have green fingers old man.

It keeps me bent over but it gives us plenty. When you come for Minnie on Tuesday I'll have a couple of cabbages and a few swedes for you.

Great, really great, I'm no gardener myself.

Almost too dark to see.

Never mind I had a good look this morning, you've got it all laid out neat as a pin. Neat as a pin old man.

And here we are.

One step away from your front door.

You can get off home for tea.

You're all right old man?

JOURNEY   63

Right as rain young fulla, couldn't be better.

I'll get along then.

Tuesday.

Now he could get in and close the door behind him and walk without limping to the lavatory because he badly needs a pee. And when he came out of the bathroom they were watching him, they were stoking up the fire and putting things on the table. They were looking at his face.

Seated at the table they were trying not to look at his face, they were trying to talk about unimportant things, there was a bad wind today and it's going to be a rough night.

Tamatea Whakapau.

It must have been cold in town.

Heaters were on in the train.

And the train, was it on time?

Right on the minute.

What about the one coming home?

Had to wait a while for the one coming home.

At the railway station, you waited at the railway station?

And I saw George.

George, how's George?

George is all right, he's just the same.

Maisie said he's joined up with a gang and he doesn't wash. She said he's got a big war sign on his jacket and won't go to work.

They get themselves into trouble she said and they all go round dirty.

George is no different, he's just the same.

They were quiet then wondering if he would say anything else, then after a while they knew he wouldn't.

But later that evening as though to put an end to some silent discussion that they may have been having he told them it wasn't safe and they weren't to put him in the ground. When I go you're not to put me in the ground, do you hear. He was an old man and his foot was giving him hell, and he was shouting at them while they sat hurting. Burn me up I tell you, it's not safe in the ground, you'll know all about it if you put me in the ground. Do you hear?

Some other time, we'll talk about it.

Some other time is now and it's all said. When I go, burn me up, no one's going to mess about with me when I'm gone.

He turned into his bedroom and shut the door. He sat on the edge of his bed for a long time looking at the palms of his hands.

COMMENTARY

'Journey' narrates an elderly man's return trip to the city of Wellington from his home in a rural area near Plimmerton (an outer suburb). He knows that such an excursion does not really warrant the name 'journey', but his choice of the word reflects the importance he attaches to his mission. He intends to speak to officials in the City Planning Department, as he needs permission to build houses for his nieces and nephews on the land his family owns. The request, previously made by his niece, has already been turned down. But as the senior member of his family, the old man, given no name in the story apart from Uncle, is confident of success.

'Journey' is remarkably flexible in the way it shifts perspective. At times the old man seems to watch himself in action, to observe himself objectively before returning to a subjective expression of his feelings and knowledge. For the most part, 'Journey' is an interior monologue expressing Uncle's memories, reasoning, intentions, opinions and careful observation: 'He better go to the lavatory because he didn't trust town lavatories, people spewed there and wrote rude words. Last time he got something stuck on his shoe. Funny people those town people.'

On occasion, the generalised pronoun 'you' is chosen: 'You could sit back and enjoy the old taxi smells of split upholstery and cigarette . . .' The point of view continues to be that of the old man, with 'you' referring to himself, while the reader can observe and identify with him. The narrative perspective does not move to other characters until the story's final eighteen lines, when members of the old man's family watch him and listen to him.

Make Lists

1 What phrases and sentences in the story express the old man's confidence in himself?

2 List the ways in which the earth has been changed or damaged to make way for roads, walkways, railways or housing.

While Patricia Grace's characterisation is skilful, attitudes to the land are the primary concern of the story. In the course of the journey by taxi and unit (inter-suburban electric train), the old man states his feelings regarding land usage. The pākehā's treatment of the land both mystifies and dismays him: 'Funny people putting their trains across the sea.' Pushing over a hill to reclaim land from the sea is a pākehā undertaking which he views with mistrust: 'The train driver knows it's not really land and he is speeding up over this strip.' The heavy machinery carving away the hillsides to create roads and housing sites produces further misgivings. Uncle speaks disparagingly of the subway and the tunnels. 'Funny people these pakehas, had to chop up everything. Couldn't talk to a hill or a tree these people, couldn't give the trees or the hills a name and make them special and leave them. Couldn't go round, only through.'

The story presents an indigenous attitude towards land. To Māori, the earth is the mother of life; its original shape and form should be respected and not harmed in any way. The old man's perception of the earth as a living being is reinforced by his description of the process of erosion: 'Then the rain'll come and the cuts will bleed for miles and the valleys will drown in blood . . .'

Such is Māori respect for the land that, for example, children may be taught to lift a stone from the seafloor, check for suitable shellfish and then return the stone to its place: 'If, in your search for shellfish, you lift a stone from its lap, return the stone to where it was' (Ihimaera 1977, p.186).

In Māori mythology, trees are the children of Tāne Mahuta. Each tree is imbued with its own spirit and its own ethos. If trees are to be cut down, it should be for good reason, so that the tree can live on in a different form—as a canoe or a carving or part of a house. Appropriate 'karakia' (prayer) traditionally accompanies any tree felling.

Most upsetting of all to the old man is the pākehā's disregard for the sacredness of cemeteries and the need for the bones of the dead to remain undisturbed, having been returned to the Earth Mother 'who welcomes and cares for those children whose earthly life has ended' (Kahukiwa & Grace 1992, p.58). He scorns the shifting of graves by pākehā to make way for a new stretch of the motorway. He had read a newspaper report which said that the graves would be relocated '*tastefully*'. Grace italicises the word to emphasise the belief that any disturbance of bones would be in the worst possible taste. At the end of the story, the old man's suggestion that he be cremated,' "burn me up" ', shocks his family since, traditionally, cremation runs counter to Māori spiritual beliefs.

The old man expresses his 'Admiration' of the pākehā's building achievement in Wellington, of 'streets and steel and concrete and asphalt and buildings miles high'. The capital 'A' and the words 'it made him tired taking it all in' suggest that 'Admiration' is ironic; his response is, in fact, quite complex.

What do you think?

1 What fault might Uncle find with the tall buildings, the concrete and the asphalt? To what extent do you agree or disagree with him?

2 Try to explain Uncle's ironical 'Admiration'.

Following the old man's resolute and confident walk from Wellington's main station towards his destination, there is a small gap in the text before the sentence: 'The railway station is a place for waiting.' It becomes clear that an interval of time has elapsed and that he is waiting for the train that will take him home. While he waits, he comments on the people coming and going, and he recalls and relives his visit to the authorities.

Discussion Topics

1 In the first two paragraphs after the break, what images, phrases or sentences indicate that Uncle's mood of optimism has gone?

2 To what extent did the official listen to the old man?

3 ' "Sir we can't always have exactly what we want . . ." ' Describe the tone of this remark. Can you find any other remarks that are similar in tone? Consider the effect of the repetition of 'Sir'.

The suggestion that land values will drop if too many Māori live in one area is insulting and expresses racial prejudice. It is also ironical, because the value of the land, in monetary terms, is of no concern to the old man. He and his family value the land because they grew up there and it is where their ancestors are buried. It is home to all members of the extended family who, though they may live elsewhere, will return as often as possible. Those continuing to live there have developed a way of life based on that land and in relation to that community.

Many details contribute to the impression that the old man is selfless and has concern for other family members and neighbours. He is not judgmental of his nephew George who drifts about the railway station. He respects George for the person he is: 'What use telling George you go empty handed and leave nothing behind, when George had always been empty handed, had never wanted anything except to have nothing.'

Close Reading of the Text

1 Consider the final eighteen lines of the story and compare them with two opening paragraphs in terms of the images chosen. Show how these reflect Uncle's mood at the beginning and at the end?

2 Why does the story conclude with Uncle 'looking at the palms of his hands'?

3 Why are so many images in 'Journey' concerned with feet and legs?

More General Discussion

1 Think of as many reasons as you can for the story's title.

2 What intentions might lie behind the planning strategies of the authorities?

3 Describe any situations comparable to this which have occurred in other parts of New Zealand, or in your country of origin, where privately owned land has been taken over by the authorities for so-called 'development'?

GLOSSARY AND NOTES

as good as gold	fine, okay
b.o.	body odour, unpleasant body smell
the cenotaph	monument erected in memory of soldiers killed in war
cripes	an expression of surprise
the early bird catches the worm	a proverb meaning that those who are early will succeed
to feel like a screwball	to feel foolish

the fingers	a rude gesture
fulla	fellow, man
a fusspot	a person who is too particular
a gang	a group of people
get-up	clothing
gog-eyed	wide-eyed
green fingers	skill in gardening, can make anything grow
jumble	short for 'jumble sale', a sale of used clothing and household items
just about done his dash	almost reached the end of his life
kai (M)	food
kēhua (M)	ghost
Kupe (M)	a legendary Māori explorer, said to be the first person to visit New Zealand
a lunatic asylum	the old-fashioned term for a hospital for the mentally ill
mates	friends
neat as a pin	very tidy
nosing into	interfering
not by a long shot	by no means, nowhere near
old blighter	old man
pākehā (M)	a European New Zealander
peeing	urinating
pipi (M)	shellfish
piss holes	smelly places, fouled by urine
pop eyes	wide surprised eyes
a proper circus	a frantic, confused situation. In this story, it means that the taxi driver has had a very busy day
right as rain	quite all right
same old	as usual

JOURNEY 71

a snotty nose	a runny nose, one that needs wiping
a sourpuss	a bad-tempered person
to spew	to vomit
'Tamatea a Ngana, Tamatea Aio, Tamatea Whakapau' (M)	the traditional belief is that the different phases of the moon generate different winds
Tāne Mahuta (M)	god of forests
the telly	the television
their old man	their father
there's nothing else to believe in	reference to the reliance on the weather reports through the media. The loss of a traditional understanding of weather patterns; this was once part of a total involvement with the earth and ancient spiritual beliefs
whacky	crazy
whakairo (M)	carvings, usually in wood
ngā whanaunga (M)	relatives, members of extended family
what's the sting?	how much money does it cost?
why to worry	why worry, it's all right
your stamping ground	the land you regard as your home. In Māori terms, this would be your ancestral land, called 'tūrangawaewae', literally the place for your own legs

KAHAWAI

From Electric City and Other Stories, 1987

KAHAWAI

All right then. One morning I got up late and hurried to the kitchen. He was up before me and would have the jug boiling, the pan plugged in, the bread popped down, I thought.

Instead he was in the front room looking out.

Because the gulls had gathered out at sea, under cloud, and were chasing, calling, falling to the water. Up, chase, drop. Screaming. There's fish, he said. It brought juices. Kahawai, beating green and silver through purple water, herding the herrings which excited the gulls, which excited me . . .

Could we . . .?
Be sick?
We could.
Have we got . . .?
Bait?
We have.
Have we got two-stroke?
No.
Get breakfast, get changed, get two-stroke.
Have we got spinners?
No. Someone borrowed.
Don't need spinners. Can trawl the heads of soldiers.
Then the others came in.
Well . . . what? Have yous got a holiday or something? Or what?
We're sick . . .
Of work.
And the fish are out there, nose to tail.
Yes, we heard.
The birds.
Saw splashes. But . . .

It's only us who don't go. Sometimes. Or don't get up. Right? Because of hangovers, or laziness, or going somewhere else. Or from not being back from somewhere. Only us have sickies. Right? But anyway . . . Good. Good on yous. Kahawai, yum. Make some bread too. Yahoo.

Lines, bait, knife, hooks, sinkers, jerseys, towel, apples, can of two-stroke, putt-putt motor, rowlocks, oars. Push the dinghy out and sidle out past the weed.

He winds the rope and pulls, tries again and then we're away putt-putting out over the navy blue, under cloud, stopping for a while to remove the sinkers from the lines and to bait the hooks with the heads of soldier fish.

Then away again to where the gulls swarm above the swarming kahawai that herd the swarming herrings. But he and I are not a swarm, we are only two of us. One fish each will do.

Then we are in the middle of it, the darting, leaping little fish crack open the dark water, leap and splash, the gull's eye singling out one, the eye of the kahawai on another. Gulls swooping, following, rising, diving, rising, swallowing, turning, following. And the kahawai zigging, zagging, leaping, shooting through the water, beating silver on the surface of it. Hundreds. But for us two will do.

We trawl our long lines with the putt-putt on slow, putt-putting through chaotic water under the screeching canopy.

Of birds. One of them is eyeing the bait, the head of the soldier, and is following. I stand spread-legged and wave one arm. No. Go. Silly bird. It's dead meat, hooked. Krazy Karoro.

Krazy Kahawai too, for that matter. And Krazy Kataha. K. K. K. And what about Krazy Kouple in a boat? K. K. K. and K.K. I wave. Shout. Go, Karoro, go. So Karoro drops back, but still follows, still wants.

And then, Got it, he says. So I stop waving, stop shouting, plonk myself down. He switches the motor off so that he can pull in . . . number one. Pulling . . .

> *What have we here ?*
> *One little kahawai, my teacher dear.*
> *Kahawai, Kahawai, nicky nicky nacky noo,*
> *That's what they taught me*
> *When I went to . . .*

Pulling . . . Pulling in over the side . . .

> *Flip flop she flied,*
> *Flip flop she flied,*
> *Flip flop she flied,*
> *She went up to heaven and flip flop she flied*
> *Flip flop she fliedy flied flied . . .*

Krazy Kahawai flapping, slapping the tin boards of the boat, bouncing in the wet sack on the tin bottom of the boat. I pull in too so that my line won't tangle in the motor while we start up again.

Off. Putt-putting full out to catch up with Karoro again. They have moved further out now, dinning and diving. We trail the heads of soldiers, turning to run with the fish . . .

> *Kahawai, Kataha, nicky nicky nacky noo,*
> *That's what they taught me . . .*
> *Hat on one side what have we here?*
> *One little chin chopper, my teacher dear.*
> *Chin chopper, snot catcher, eye basher, sweaty boxer,*
> *   nicky nacky noo*
> *That's what they taught me when . . .*

Karoro. Again. Eyeing, swooping. I stand, wave, shout. Not for you. Shoo. Wave and shout. Go. Blow. Karoro backs off, then moves up again. I pick up an apple, throw it, and Karoro turns, circles, returns. Krazy Kamikaze Karoro. I pick up the towel, swing it, and Karoro, nervous, drops back, still wanting, still turning the eye.

But then, is beaten to the bait by Kahawai. Number two. Got it. He switches off and I sit down pulling in swiftly . . .

> *One little kahawai my teacher dear,*
> *Kahawai, Kahawai, nicky nicky nacky noo,*
> *That's what they taught me when . . .*
> *Kahawai, Kahawai, nicky nicky nacky noo,*
> *That's what they . . .*
> *What have we here?*
> *One great big kahawai my teacher dear,*
> *Kahawai, Karoro, Kataha, Krazy Kouple, nicky nicky*
>   *nacky noo,*
> *That's what they taught me . . .*

Bring it in over the side, hand into the gills, push the hook. Look Karoro, hook, turn your eye. Not meant, not bent for a feathered throat. Open the bag and . . .

> *Flip flop she flied,*
> *Flip flop she flied,*
> *Flip flop she flied,*
> *She went up to heaven and flip flop she flied*
> *Flip flop she fliedy flied flied.*

And now, the gulls, the fish have moved out again, too far for a tin boat and a putt-putt on a cold day. It's Kold, and two will do. One flick and we're moving again, turning, the Krazy Kouple. Kold. Heading home.

As we come to the weed in the shallow water we switch off, lifting the motor, and row in swiftly. Kold. We step out, ahh, into water, kold hands gripping the sides of the boat. Can we lift it? We can, rushing it up over the stones. Rest, then again. Again, blue knuckled. And lift. Can we? On to the trailer? We can.

Then back to the edge we go with the two fish, scraping fast, because it's kold. The scales leap. We slit the white bellies, pulling the insides out, flinging. Kum Karoro. They come, dance on the surface of the sea, snatch the innards and fly up gulping. We wash the fish and the water runs red-salt-blood. We hurry with the trailer, home, to be dry and warm.

When it is time I put bread in the oven. He cuts up fish, puts it in the big pot with a good fist of salt, watches so that it won't boil fast. We scrub and slice vegetables and put them on to cook.

Then the others come, lifting the lids of the pots. Did yous? Yous did.

Opening the oven door.

Did yous? Yous did. Yum.

When it is time we lift the fish carefully into bowls and strain the water into a jug. We break up the bread on the board and heap the vegetables on to dishes.

Then we sit down to celebrate.

COMMENTARY

This story, Patricia Grace has said, is based on a real occasion when she and her husband went fishing instead of going to work. There is good understanding between the couple who decide to make the most of the fact that a school of kahawai is out in the bay. The activity of the gulls indicates what is happening beneath the surface: 'Kahawai, beating green and silver through the purple water, herding the herrings which excited the gulls, which excited me . . .' Arrangements are made swiftly. Such is the understanding between man and wife that only single words and fragments of sentences are needed.

Read Aloud

In groups of four, read aloud the first thirty-three lines of the story. Divide the reading task carefully: Man, Wife, Others One and Two.

The couple intend to catch only two fish: 'One fish each will do.' Traditional respect for the sea dictates that Māori take only as much seafood as they need; fish may be caught in quantity if the surplus is carefully preserved by boiling and drying or by smoking. To families living by the sea, seafood has always been an important part of their diet. Nothing would be wasted.

Pace is achieved by the use of many action words, 'darting, leaping little fish crack open the dark water . . .' The intense, repetitive rhythm creates a mood of high excitement: 'And the kahawai zigging, zagging, leaping, shooting . . .' While the gulls screech and dive, the couple haul in fish, and chant jingles. The gulls' assault and the narrator's attempt to ward them off is likened to a boxing match: ' "Chin chopper, snot catcher, eye basher, sweaty boxer . . ." ' and turned into an incantation:

Kahawai, Kataha, nicky nicky nacky noo,
That's what they taught me . . .
Hat on one side what have we here?

One little chin chopper, my teacher dear,
Chin chopper, snot catcher, eye basher, sweaty boxer,
  nicky nacky noo
That's what they taught me when . . .

The jingles give the impression of playfulness and enjoyment. So, too, do the many words beginning with 'k'. In the Māori alphabet, there is a 'k' but no 'c'. Grace uses the Māori names: 'karoro' (gull), 'kataha' (herring) and 'kahawai'; and spells a number of familiar English words with 'k' rather than 'c': 'krazy', 'kouple', 'kold', 'kum'. The words become part of the noisy exchange of gull cries, and the calling, chanting, shouting of the couple: 'Krazy Kamikaze Karoro'. The cries of the gulls, more often written in English as 'Kaa, Kaa, Kaa' are expressed as the urgent outburst 'K.K.K.'.

If, at the outset, we were unsure whether the narrator was male or female, the concluding paragraphs make it clear. The couple work as a team to prepare the meal. The raw fish is cut up by the man. The bread-making, traditionally a woman's task, is carried out by the narrator. They share the preparation of the vegetables.

The Māori idiom 'yous' is used in this story. The ambiguity of 'you' has long been a frustration to those for whom English is a second language. The solution for many Māori speakers has been to add an 's' to indicate the plural meaning. In contrast to English, the Māori pronouns signifying 'you' are very precise, indicating one, two, three or more people.

The story concludes with a celebration. Having cooked their fish, made bread and cooked vegetables, the two sit down to eat their meal. They are joined by 'others' who will share it. A celebration in the Māori world is no celebration at all without sharing, a value which is fundamental in traditional Māori culture. It is basic to 'whanaungatanga', which is a code of support and loyalty among members of any 'whānau' or group linked by kinship or friendship. Sharing is equally important to the concept of 'manaakitanga' which names the quality of care and respect extended to guests.

In 'Kahawai' the reader plays a vital part in completing the story by filling in the gaps, ' "When I went to . . . " ', by interpreting the 'c' words spelt with 'k', and by finishing the sentence fragments, ' "Could we . . .?" ' The reader is called upon to take part in the chaotic action: to ward off the gulls as they dive, to join in the triumphant verse chanting and to share the delicious meal.

Focus on Language

1 List the words expressing (a) the action of the gulls; (b) the action of the fish; (c) the action of the couple.

2 Look at the use of short sentences, parts of sentences, single words, action words and repetition, all of which contribute to the pace. Which words contribute most to the sense of excitement?

3 Discuss the effect of the tenses chosen for this story.

GLOSSARY AND NOTES

blow	go away!
chin chopper	metaphor likening a gull to a boxing opponent
flied	flew
K.K.K.	Kaa Kaa Kaa, the call of gulls
kahawai (M)	a type of fish, generally caught where the river mouth runs into the sea
Kamikaze	metaphor likening a gull to a pilot prepared to crash
karoro (M)	seagull
kataha (M)	herring, a small fish, food of the kahawai
manaakitanga (M)	care and respect to visitors, hospitality
nicky nicky nacky noo	nonsense words

plonk	sit down abruptly
putt-putt	sound of an outboard motor (on the dinghy)
screeching canopy	metaphor suggesting many gulls overhead
sickies	sick leave taken when people are well
spinner	silvery lures with hooks at the end that look like fish
two-stroke	oil and petrol fuel mix
whānau (M)	group linked by kinship or friendship
whanaugatanga (M)	kinship, relationships in the extended family
Yahoo	noisy expression of delight
yous	idiom for plural of you

OLD ONES BECOME BIRDS

From The Sky People, 1994

OLD ONES BECOME BIRDS

She thought of bedsocks like the ones she'd seen at the Martinborough Fair, knitted in double bluegreen—stockingstitch in the foot, patterned above, with crocheted drawstrings threaded round the ankles. Same pattern as baby booties, only large. Had thought of buying a pair but it was summer then.

The light near the door was on but the rest of the house was dark and beginning to snore. Woman on the mattress on one side of her was tuning up, and on the other side was an old wheezer. Oldies all having early nights. She settled into the sleeping bag trying not to rustle. Rugby socks would've done the trick.

Anyway she was pleased to have found a space in the main sleeping house, knowing that out in the 'barracks' the young ones would be up talking half the night—preparing workshops or just fooling about. Even now she could hear them coming and going, singing, laughing. But only sounds. Far enough away to be soothing as she lay rubbing blood down into her feet. In the morning some of them would be out doing aerobics with Gus. In the morning there'd be ice.

The birds started up, but that was later. Before that, before light, in the deep morning, the tuner next to her began rattling her baggage and murmuring to her companion on the far side. The two put on coats and began making their way, feeling each footstep, chatting loud enough for their own old ears about a torch that one of them had and who it belonged to originally and who that person's father and mother were, and who the grandparents were and where they were originally from. The door opened. No light to come in through it but soon there was torchlight jigging away in the direction of the washroom.

By the time the two returned the coughing had started, the talk, the movement to sit up and wait for light, the to-ing and fro-ing in the dark to the showers, whizzing of atomisers. The women made their way in and got back in under their quilts to wait. The shower was good and hot it seemed.

On the other side of her the old wheezer was pulling on socks, putting a coat over his pyjamas and she expected he was going for a shower too. But no, he was making his way to a space between the window and door, tapping the pou and beginning to chant the morning karakia. Around the house others were joining in, picking up for him when his breath ran out, these first birds.

She knew they wouldn't be let off lightly with the invocations, which seemed timeless and unending and so early old bird. Restful once she'd accepted that there'd be no more sleep for her that morning. She closed her eyes and let the singsong wash, and when she opened them again dawn had been canted in. She lay and waited for full light.

Hard frost, and a few out with Gus doing aerobics guitar-style. Then a cold shower that she was not keen enough to get right under, but she washed and put on most of the clothing she'd brought with her. Back out in the white she found two mates to walk with before breakfast, comparing nights and the state of showers.

They walked in a white world, along white tracks, through white paddocks, by white fenceposts wired silver. Cobwebs in filigree. Glass trees. Her words were carried on white breath telling of the early-early birds, and back on white breath came the telling about the night in the barracks that had been noisy and cold. One of her companions had managed to sleep through it, one hadn't. Sky of steel with sun burning a white hole in it.

Seating had been arranged in front of the meeting house and the old ones had already found their places. They were animated, chirpy, turning their faces to the sun as they waited for the unveiling of the carved stone which was the first event on the programme for the day. Once the words had been said and the kakahu removed the olds led them all by the carved piece so they could all see and touch it. She watched them ahead of her as they clutched about them their coloured shawls and rugs, fluffing them featherly, beaking the ground with their sticks, eyeing from side to side, feet big and spread in hugboots, ugboots, gumboots and shoes.

At the main meeting of the day the elders had a great deal to say on the subject of oral histories. Stories, if that's what it meant. Life, if that's what it meant. Yeh, yeh, they don't mind telling the stories, long as the stories don't get stolen so all those Pakehas go and make money. And don't want their stories thieved by all those archive people too. It's for our own. That's that. Our own mokopuna. Don't want our own people ripping us off too, it's for the kids.

By afternoon the heads were dropping wingward, the birdlids beginning to droop over bird eyes. Up to everybody else those other things—recommendations, delegations, applications, justifications. Had enough of that but we support the idea, the recording of stories so the children will know. Otherwise, if we didn't support it wouldn't be here with a rumatiki and a flu, middle of winter, telling it.

After a while she realised many of the seats were empty. There'd been a quiet exit of olds. In on the mattresses for an hour or two before mealtime she guessed.

Or gone flying

She looked up. Yes, there they all were in their bird colours.

Become birds.

There, beating up into the sky that deepened as their many-coloured wings blocked the sun, while from their throats came the chatter, taptap, call, chant, scratch, wheeze.

It wasn't long before she felt herself rising.

COMMENTARY

Patricia Grace chose to read 'Old Ones Become Birds' during Writers and Readers Week, at the New Zealand International Festival of the Arts, in Wellington, March 1996. She explained that the story was occasioned by a mid-winter visit to the Omaka Marae near Blenheim. The audience's appreciative laughter sprang from recognition of the events which this story captures.

But readers who have never stayed on a 'marae' may be somewhat puzzled. The 'house' referred to is a meeting house. A third-person narrator describes it as: 'dark and beginning to snore.' 'Woman on the mattress on one side of her was tuning up, and on the other side an old wheezer.' 'Oldies all having early nights.' The situation is well known to all who have enjoyed this remarkable form of hospitality and accommodation. In this particular case, potential difficulties take a somewhat extreme form because so many elderly are together at one time.

A gathering of many people on a marae for the purpose of discussion or celebration is called a 'hui'. In 'Old Ones Become Birds', the hui has been called to decide whether to allow the divulging of oral histories to Māori children—or to a wider audience.

The meeting house is the focus of social life in a Māori community. In *Potiki*, Patricia Grace describes its functions in the following way: 'the people's place of resting, their place of learning, of discussing, singing, dancing, sorrow, joy, renewal, and whanaungatanga' (Grace 1986, p.136). 'Whanaungatanga' is the concept of family ties, support and loyalty among those who are members of the same extended family. When visitors have been welcomed on to the marae, they also become part of the extended family and enjoy the care and support implicit in whanaungatanga and required by the principles of 'manaakitanga' (hospitality).

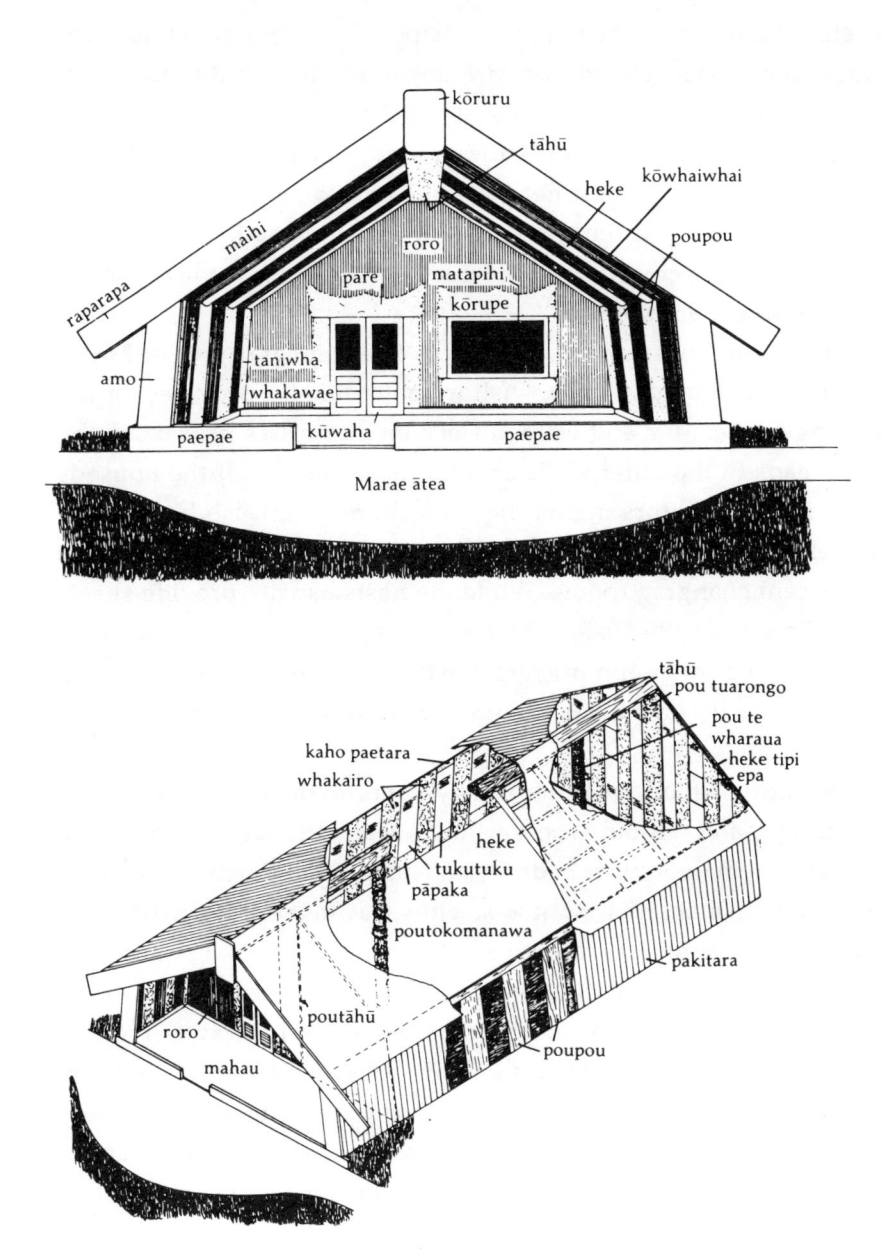

Figure 1: The whare whakairo (Tanenuiarangi, The University of Auckland)

Meeting houses are rectangular in shape with a deep porch in front where footwear is left, so that dirt, anger and negativity can be left outside; the house is a place of peace. Above the porch, arms (or barge boards) angled towards the ground, stretch out in welcome. In most cases, the carved head at the apex of the arms represents the ancestor after whom the house has been named. The house is likened to a protective parent, in which the ridgepole is the backbone and the rafters are the ribs.

Caring for, and respecting, visitors is an integral part of Māori culture. Accommodation for visitors is frequently provided in the meeting house. Men and women sleep on mattresses placed side by side, heads to the outer walls around the perimeter. If the house is large and the visitors many, the central area may also be used by sleepers. Guests change into night attire and dressing gowns or coats in adjacent changing rooms. While the hosts usually provide sheets and pillow cases, the visitors bring sleeping bags, quilts or blankets. After evening songs and prayers, the house settles for the night. But, as 'Old Ones Become Birds' shows, the settling may not be achieved easily.

The central character is flanked by a snorer, the woman who 'was tuning up', and 'an old wheezer', who was asthmatic. Elderly folk can rarely remain in their beds for an entire night, but must extricate themselves to make their not-too-stealthy way to the toilet. Experience has made them aware, moreover, that those who take showers at four in the morning will find them good and hot. The restless sleeper in Grace's story hears her neighbours making their way to the exit door in the small hours, 'chatting loud enough for their own old ears about a torch that one of them had and who it belonged to originally and who the person's father and mother were, and who the grandparents were and where they were originally from.' Reminiscences about family connections are typical at such gatherings.

Sleep is disturbed, not only by those shuffling out and shuffling back to their places, but also by the early 'karakia' or prayer. (No morning in the meeting house begins without it.) Some people move to sit close by the minister or elder. Some people join in the chanting from their mattresses, while others sleep on.

'The olds' have a collective character, and their particular needs are occasioned by their age. In the formal discussion which takes place later in the day, they have very definite opinions which they offer, before resolving to leave to 'everybody else those other things—recommendations, delegations, applications, justifications. Had enough of that but we support the idea, the recording of stories so the children will know.' Grace captures with accuracy the way the elderly speak their minds.

The central character observes with sympathetic amusement the contribution of the olds who have come despite 'a rumatiki and a flu, middle of winter . . .' Throughout the story, the elderly are compared to birds. Walking sticks are 'beaking the ground' and coloured shawls and rugs are likened to plumage. As they became weary in the afternoon, their 'heads were drooping wingward'. Such a comparison is well known and generally complimentary. This metaphor is one of the many that would be immediately recognised by speakers of Māori, since Māori orators and writers are habitually metaphoric and frequently draw upon a pool of familiar images.

The story concludes with an element of fantasy as the olds are thought to have transformed themselves into birds in flight. But there is more to the image than mere fantasy. It is believed that the 'wairua' or spirit of the dead may take the form of small birds to visit those of this world. Since the elderly have disappeared from the gathering, it is imagined that they have, in the meantime, become birds, perhaps communing with those who have died. As one of the privileges of their advanced years, they may be capable of moving back and forth between this world and the next.

Discussion Topics

1. What can you discover about the temperament of the central character?

2. What indication is there that 'the olds' are suspicious of most people? Are they simply being unreasonable? Why do you think they are not more trusting?

3. Share suggestions as to why the early morning walk in a white world is important to the story. (There is no right or wrong answer here.)

4. The last line is a significant statement. How do you understand it? (The word 'rising' has at least two meanings.)

5. Imagine yourself at this hui among those who stayed on the marae overnight. What might you have learnt?

GLOSSARY AND NOTES

barracks	makeshift accommodation like that used by soldiers
canted in	brought in with the incantations
hugboots, ugboots	large fur or fleece-lined boots
hui (M)	gathering, meeting
kākahu (M)	finely woven cloak
karakia (M)	prayer
manaakitanga (M)	care and respect to visitors, hospitality
marae (M)	meeting-ground
mates	friends
mokopuna (M)	grandchildren, descendants who are children
olds, oldies	elderly people

oral histories	the history of the Māori is almost all oral. Traditionally, the knowledge was possessed by senior people and passed on to selected descendants
pou (M)	post, pole
ripping us off	taking advantage of us
rūmātiki (M)	rheumatism
tuning up	starting to snore
whanaungatanga (M)	kinship, relationships in the extended family
wheezer	asthmatic

SUN'S MARBLES

From The Sky People, 1994

SUN'S MARBLES

When Maui booby-trapped Sun then clobbered him over the head with a hunk of bone shaped like two parts of a bootmaker's last, he won, for all time, high praise as the pioneer of daylight saving.

It was a surprise attack.

It was a violent act.

During the beating, which was resolute and prolonged, Sun lost some of his marbles, most of which went skittering out to stardom. Some, however, dropped to Earth, who caught them tidily, although she didn't really want them because she understood that these pretty things could be dangerous. But she was stuck with them. She couldn't send them back because Gravity was so lopsided, so she hid them deep in her pockets.

Earth had an instinct for hiding things. In the early days when she and Sky were close together, hiddenness had been a way of life. Everything had been hidden between these two. Light could not penetrate and there was no room to swing a cat's ancestor.

There was no 'above' and 'below' in those days. No direction was different from any other no—'vertical', 'horizontal' or 'diagonal' as Earth and Sky rolled together in each other's arms. Or alternatively, every position was above or below, every direction was north, south, east and west, every angle was vertical, horizontal or diagonal. But there was no superiority and Challenge had not been born, even though there was an inkling of it in the minds of some of Earth and Sky's children. There was the potential.

Parents speak to each other in double language, spell out secrets so that children will not understand what they are talking about. But children get an inkling, if not of the content of the secret, then at least of the idea that there is a secret, something to be discovered, to be gleaned from whisperings if they keep on listening in the dark, keep adding one little piece of nothingness to another.

Earth and Sky were born out of Darkness and therefore knew about Light, and this was the secret they wanted to keep to themselves so that their children would remain children, keep their innocence and stay with them forever.

But the children were patient listeners, and blind, innocent and squashed between their ever-embracing parents as they were, they got to talking. The listeners and decoders of secret language among them had worked out that there was something else. There was something being kept from them by their parents and they would not be satisfied until they found out what it was. It was to do with otherness, other realms, the other side. It was when the children first talked to each other about these matters that Dissatisfaction was first expressed, but not clearly expressed and not clearly understood.

What came out of the discussion was that there was a desire by most of the children to have greater understanding. If they were to have greater understanding, then their known world had to be changed.

They had to get outside of it somehow, but they were bound on all sides by the locked bodies of their parents. They were squashed and breathless and realised they would have to separate their parents if they were to become free. How were they to do this from their position of powerlessness?

There were Plants, but none of them were upright and were only as vines creeping about in the dark. There was Water, but it was stagnated and lifeless. There was Wind, but it was only as stale breath. Conflict, being a metaphor for People, was only the beginnings of an idea.

So the offspring of Sky and Earth began trying to move the parents away from each other, pushing, pulling, prising, but were not successful until Plant Life stopped creeping about, tried standing, then just kept on doing what it normally did—that is, grow—but from a different perspective. That's when Perspective and Direction began to be understood. After some eras Sky was lifted off Earth by upwardly mobile Plant Life and the children found out about Light.

Wind had been the dissenter from all this, and after the big event became angry with all those who had had anything to do with separating his mother and father. So he called up northerlies, southerlies, easterlies, westerlies, nor'westers, sou'easters, storms, hurricanes and tornadoes—and stirred up chaos amongst Plants and Waters and the Creatures who, now that there was Light and Space, had been released among them.

It was while Wind was having his tantrums that Earth realised that some of her kids needed protection against others, and she did her best to hide some of the less protected ones until it was safe for them to come out again. She had fought long and hard against being separated from Sky, but now that it was done she was determined to make the best of the situation.

Well, all this Light. All this Space. It was almost too much of a good thing. Plants and Creatures spread everywhere. Water became seas, lakes and rivers, and became inhabited by Swimmers. Eventually People made an appearance, but this didn't happen without a great deal of trauma, which included incest, personality change, family break-up and solo parenthood.

In spite of all this Earth and Sky did the best they could to be good providers. They tried to take an interest in what was happening.

When the latest addition came along, these People, Earth and Sky were fascinated and pleased and thought that living apart and allowing Light and Space had some compensations after all. In fact they indulged these latest offspring, gave them free rein, but soon found that the more they were given the more they wanted.

These Johnny-come-latelies reckoned life would be better if they had a bit more daytime, even though they were told they should be grateful for what they had. In the olden days their ancestors had had no daylight at all. This kind of talk fell on deaf ears.

Anyhow, Maui was the one who took up the cause on People's behalf. Maui was a foundling, who in his formative years hadn't known his true parentage; and he was born ugly, which didn't help matters. But to offset these seeming disadvantages he was of impeccable stock and had a mother who saw opportunities and was prepared to give him up at birth in order that his gifts be allowed to develop. Also he was part human—a combination of Worldly and Other Worldly—so it was appropriate that he should be the one to act as a go-between for People.

In taking up the challenge to lengthen daylight he beat up Sun so badly that Sun hobbled about like an old koroua and from then on took many hours to travel across the face of Sky.

And that was when Earth, seeing the beating handed out to Sun, hid Sun's marbles away because she knew instinctively that they would be dangerous in the wrong hands. She knew that these latest, very demanding offspring were not mature enough to take responsibility for them.

Later on, this same Maui, who must have learned Irresponsibility from the human side of his genealogy, went to get Fire for his earthly cousins. Because of the immature way he handled the situation, Fire had to be sent to hide in the bodies of trees so that Maui and these earthlings wouldn't play fast and loose with it.

Anyway, these Teina, younger sisters and brothers of Winds, Waters, Plants, Animals, Birds, Insects, Reptiles and Fish, were really too big for their boots. Upstarts. In many ways they took after Maui, being Potiki, last born. Like Maui they had outsized attitude problems and didn't care what happened or who got hurt as long as they got their own way.

These ones had no idea of how to look after their own best interests either, and without the approval of those more mature and knowledgeable than themselves, began to change the order of things.

They began to kill their Tuakana—that is, their older brothers and sisters—without good reason, and to destroy their living places. The more powerful ones among them stole food and took over the living places of the less powerful ones of their own tribe too.

And they weren't satisfied with that. They'd heard about Sun's marbles and that Earth had hidden them somewhere. They knew they'd never be happy until they found them, and they began to search. They made great holes all over Earth, shifting or destroying Plants and Animals as well as the powerless members of their own tribe.

At last they found Sun's marbles in Earth's deepest pockets and with these they made objects in their own likeness—that is, they made objects capable of enormous destruction that were not able to be properly controlled. During the making of these objects there was so much waste that many of their own tribe had to be shifted away from their homes to make room for it, many had to run in fear of it. Many had nowhere to go and had to live with it. They became ill and maimed, gave birth to sick children, died painfully.

Sun could do nothing on the day when he rose, unaware, and was straitjacketed by Maui's snare. And when that bone came cracking down on him, chipping off bits, he could only hold tight and hope his days weren't ended.

Sky is no butterfingers and was deft in gathering in Sun's marbles, and though it was no accident that he allowed a few to go Earthward, he later came to regret this.

It was instinct that caused Earth to tuck these bright things away. Neither she nor Sky realised at the time that their children could become their enemies, or that they themselves could be enslaved. They were indulgent parents inclined to put unacceptable behaviour down to teething problems, hyperactivity, high intelligence or precocity.

But later they began to ask themselves where they'd gone wrong. Was it because of their separation that these children had become so grasping, so out of control? Had Sky been too distant? Had Earth been too over-compensating? What could they have done about it anyway? Was it all a question of Light?

COMMENTARY

'Sun's Marbles' is humorous in manner, but serious in theme. The story retells sections of well-known myths and then deliberately transforms them, altering the events and consequences we anticipate, perhaps to encourage some careful thought about our collective actions and responsibilities.

Instead of the dignified, formal language usually deemed suitable for relating myths, Patricia Grace chooses familiar and colloquial language. With the conversational manner of an oral storyteller, she brings ancient patterns of cause and effect into a contemporary context. Thus the old and the new come together with surprising effect.

'Sun's Marbles' begins with the story of how Māui snared the sun. Three skilful sentences suffice for Patricia Grace's retelling. She includes casual idioms: clobbered, booby-trapped, hunk; and she introduces a modern concept, day-light saving. In Māui's time, people complained about the shortness of each day. Māui's solution was to 'beat up the Sun so badly that Sun hobbled about like an old koroua and from then on took many hours to travel across the face of Sky.' Grace's account is in accordance with the myth, but she chooses the modern idiom 'to beat up', meaning to cause grievous injury, deliberately.

Having dealt with the original, familiar event, Grace introduces something new: 'During the beating . . . Sun lost some of his marbles . . .' To 'lose some marbles', another contemporary idiom, suggests damage to the mind—usually through age or injury. But, to the reader's amusement, Grace uses the expression literally. Some of the marbles, valuable and beautiful, drop to Earth. Aware of their value and danger, Earth hides them deep in her pockets to protect her children. The myth has taken an unexpected direction.

The story then moves back in time to a second myth. During the aeons in which Earth and Sky were 'rolled together in each other's arms', their children were imprisoned in the dark and confined space between the parents where 'there was no room to swing a cat's ancestor.'

In Grace's story, the children of Earth and Sky become like young people of any age, aware of 'double language' expressing 'secrets so that children will not understand what they are talking about.' The parents were hiding the secret of 'Light'.

In retelling the myth of the children's dissatisfaction, Grace names them, not according to their mythical names, but according to their realms of responsibility: Plant Life (Tāne Mahuta); Water (Tangaroa); Wind (Tawhirimatea) and Conflict (Tūmatauenga). Tāne Mahuta finally succeeds in separating his parents: 'With a powerful thrust of his legs he levered upward, and Papa hurtled away from Rangi' (Mataira 1975, p.8). Grace's version is as follows: 'After some eras, Sky was lifted off Earth by upwardly mobile Plant Life and the children found out about Light.'

Discussion Topic
'Upwardly mobile' is a contemporary catch-phrase. What does it mean, figuratively and literally?

Further reference to mythology is made when Grace writes: 'Eventually, People made an appearance, but this didn't happen without a great deal of trauma, which included incest, personality change, family break-up and solo parenthood.' These present-day problems have their counterparts in mythology. Tāne Mahuta pursued his own daughter, the beautiful Hine-titama, abandoning his wife, Hine-ahu-one, the first woman. The result was the first 'family break-up'; 'incest' and 'personality change' followed. Tāne and his daughter became parents, but, according to one version of the myth, when Hine-titama found that her husband was also her father, she descended in shame into the underworld to become the Great Lady of the Night, Hine-nui-te-Pō.

'Sun's Marbles' moves from mythical events to the behaviour of people expressed in terms of contemporary jargon: they became 'too big for their boots' and they developed 'outsized attitude problems', both idioms signifying arrogance and irresponsibility. Having heard about the treasured marbles, they made holes in the earth and destroyed plants, animals and other people. As in 'Journey', it is clear that the story teller regards any damage to the Earth Mother—drilling, blasting, tunnelling—to be disrespectful and offensive.

Make a List

Which words or images express the narrator's sense of outrage at damage to the earth?

When the marbles were found, the people created 'objects in their own likeness—that is, they made objects capable of enormous destruction that were not able to be properly controlled'. Grace takes the biblical concept that 'God created man in his *own* image' (Genesis 2:7), and uses the idea in an original manner. Man and the weapons of destruction are not alike in any superficial way. They have one thing in common, both are destructive by nature.

While it may seem flippant on the surface, 'Sun's Marbles' is serious in meaning. It is an allegorical story, referring back to well-known stories, and distorting them in deliberate, often amusing ways. The result may be that we see our own behaviour in a different context, or that we adopt a more critical view of familiar patterns of conduct. While parables spell out a lesson, modern allegories are usually ambiguous; they tend to awaken critical thinking.

Sky and Earth become like many of today's parents, concerned at the behaviour of their children and asking themselves 'where they'd gone wrong.' The final question 'Was it all a question of Light?' can provoke many answers, since light can mean enlightenment or knowledge. A parallel can be drawn between the biblical idea of the 'Fall of Man', once he lost his innocence and gained knowledge (Genesis 3:4), and the coming of light into the space beween Rangi and Papatūānuku.

Discussion Topics

1 Under two headings, list the kind of knowledge which you consider dangerous and the kind of knowledge you consider essential.

2 How can young people be protected from dangerous knowledge while gaining the expertise necessary for life in the modern world?

3 If you take the position that the Earth is our Mother, what would be your attitude:

(a) to the way she is treated, and

(b) to the way her children treat one another?

4 How do you respond to the suggestion that the inhabitants of the Earth have, for centuries, acted like irresponsible children?

5 To what extent are parents responsible for the misbehaviour of their children?

GLOSSARY AND NOTES

booby-trapped	a snare deliberately set to make a victim look foolish
bootmaker's last	a metal form on which a boot or shoe is placed for making or repair
butterfingers	person who drops or fails to catch things
clobbered	hit
daylight saving	putting the clock forward an hour over summer to make the most of the hours of daylight
earthlings	earth people
fell on deaf ears	was not acknowledged

gleaned	picked up in the form of little bits and pieces
a go-between	a mediator
hunk	large slab
an inkling	a vague notion about something
Johnny-come-latelies	newcomers
koroua (M)	old man
the latest addition	youngest child
no room to swing a cat's ancestor	the familiar saying is 'there is no room to swing a cat'
Papatūānuku (M)	the Earth Mother, in Māori mythology
play fast and loose	take liberties
pōtiki (M)	the youngest child in a family
Rangi (M)	the Sky Father, in Māori mythology
skittering	slipping and sliding
straitjacketed	trapped. A straitjacket is used for restraining mentally ill patients.
Tāne Mahuta (M)	god of forests, in Māori mythology
Tangaroa (M)	god of the sea, in Māori mythology
Tawhirimatea (M)	god of winds, in Māori mythology
teina (M)	younger brothers and sisters
too big for their boots	arrogant
they had outsized attitude problems	inconsiderate and badly behaved people
tuākana (M)	older brothers and sisters
Tūmatauenga (M)	god of war, in Māori mythology
upstarts	inexperienced and over confident
upwardly mobile	improving social status
Worldly and Other Worldly	descended from the world of humans and from the spirit world (from the gods)

NGATI KANGARU

From The Sky People, 1994

NGATI KANGARU

Billy was laughing his head off reading the history of the New Zealand Company, har, har, har, har.

It was since he'd been made redundant from Mitre 10 that he'd been doing all this reading. Billy and Makere had four children, one who had recently qualified as a lawyer but was out of work, one in her final year at university, and two at secondary school. These kids ate like elephants. Makere's job as a checkout operator for New World didn't bring in much money and she thought Billy should be out looking for another job instead of sitting on his backside all day reading and laughing.

The book belonged to Rena, whose full given names were Erena Meretiana. She wanted the book back so she could work on her assignment. Billy had a grip on it.

Har, har, these Wakefields were real crooks. That's what delighted Billy. He admired them, and at the beginning of his reading had been distracted for some minutes while he reflected on that first one, E. G. Wakefield, sitting in the clink studying up on colonisation. Then by the time of his release, EG had the edge on all those lords, barons, MPs, lawyers and so forth. Knew more about colonisation than they did, haaar.

However, Billy wasn't too impressed with the reason for EG's incarceration. Abducting an heiress? Jeepers! Billy preferred more normal, more cunning crookery, something funnier—like lying, cheating and stealing.

So in that regard he wasn't disappointed as he read on, blobbed out in front of the two-bar heater that was expensive to run, Makere reminded him. Yes, initial disappointment left him the more he progressed in his reading. Out-and-out crooks, liars, cheats and thieves, these Wakefields. He felt inspired.

What he tried to explain to Makere was that he wasn't just spending his time idly while he sat there reading. He was learning a few things from EG, WW, Jerningham, Arthur and Co., that would eventually be of benefit to him as well as to the whole family. He knew it in his bones.

'Listen to this,' he'd say, as Makere walked in the door on feet that during the course of the day had grown and puffed out over the tops of her shoes. And he'd attempt to interest her with excerpts from what he'd read. ' "The Wakefields' plan was based on the assumption that vast areas—if possible, every acre—of New Zealand would be bought for a trifle, the real payment to the people of the land being their 'civilising' . . . " Hee hee, that's crafty. They called it "high and holy work".

'And here. There was this "exceptional Law" written about in one of EG's anonymous publications, where chiefs sold a heap of land for a few bob and received a section "in the midst of emigrants" in return. But har, har, the chiefs weren't allowed to live on this land until they had "learned to estimate its value". Goodby-ee, don't cry-ee. It was held in reserve waiting for the old fellas to be brainy enough to know what to do with it.

'Then there was this "adopt-a-chief scheme", a bit like the "dial-a-kaumatua" scheme that they have today where you bend some old bloke's ear for an hour or two, let him say a few wise words and get him to do the old rubber-stamp trick, hee, hee. Put him up in a flash hotel and give him a ride in an aeroplane then you've consulted with every iwi throughout Aotearoa, havintcha? Well, "adopt-a-chief" was a bit the same except the prizes were different. They gave out coats of arms, lessons in manners and how to mind your p's and q's, that sort of stuff. I like it. You could do anything as long as you had a "worthy cause",' and Billy would become pensive. 'A worthy cause. Orl yew need is a werthy caws.'

On the same day that Billy finished reading the book he found his worthy cause. He had switched on television to watch *Te Karere*, when the face of his first cousin Hiko, who lived in Poi Hakena, Australia, came on to the screen.

The first shots showed Hiko speaking to a large rally of Maori people in Sydney who had formed a group called Te Hokinga ki Aotearoa. This group was in the initial stages of planning for a mass return of Maori to their homeland.

In the interview that followed, Hiko explained that there was disillusionment among Maori people with life in Australia and that they now wanted to return to New Zealand. Even the young people who had been born in Australia, who may never have seen Aotearoa, were showing an interest in their ancestral home. The group included three or four millionaires, along with others who had made it big in Oz, as well as those on the bones of their arses—or that's how Billy translated into English what Hiko had said in Maori, to Hana and Gavin. These two were Hana Angeline and Gavin Rutene, the secondary schoolers, who had left their homework to come and gog at their uncle on television.

Hiko went on to describe what planning would be involved in the first stage of The Return, because this transfer of one hundred families was a first stage only. The ultimate plan was to return all Maori people living in Australia to Aotearoa, iwi by iwi. But the groups didn't want to come home to nothing, was what Hiko was careful to explain. They intended all groups to be well housed and financed on their return, and discussions and decisions on how to make it all happen were in progress. Billy's ears prickled when Hiko began to speak of the need for land, homes, employment and business ventures. ' "Possess yourselves of the soil," ' he muttered, ' "and you are secure." '

Ten minutes later he was on the phone to Hiko.

By the time the others returned—Makere from work, Tu from job-hunting and Rena from varsity—Billy and the two children had formed a company, composed a rap, cleared a performance space in front of the dead fireplace, put their caps on backwards and practised up to performance standard:

First you go and form a Co.
Make up lies and advertise
Buy for a trifle the land you want
For Jew's harps, nightcaps
Mirrors and beads

Sign here sign there
So we can steal
And bring home cuzzies
To their 'Parent Isle'

Draw up allotments on a map
No need to buy just occupy
Rename the places you now own
And don't let titles get you down
For blankets, fish hooks, axes and guns
Umbrellas, sealing wax, pots and clothes

Sign here, sign there
So we can steal
And bring home cuzzies
To their 'Parent Isle'

Bought for a trifle sold for a bomb
Homes for your rellies
And dollars in the bank
Bought for a trifle sold for a bomb
Homes for your rellies and
Dollars in the bank

Ksss Aue, Aue,
Hi.

Billy, Hana and Gavin bowed to Makere, Tu and Rena. 'You are looking at a new company,' Billy said. 'which from henceforward (his vocabulary had taken on some curiosities since he had begun reading histories) will be known as Te Kamupene o Te Hokinga Mai.'

'Tell Te Kamupene o Te Hokinga Mai to cough up for the mortgage,' said Makere, disappearing offstage with her shoes in her hand.

'So all we need,' said Billy to Makere, later in the evening, is a vast area of land "as far as the eye can see".'

'Is that all?' said Makere.

'Of "delightful climate" and "rich soil" that is "well watered and coastal". Of course it'll need houses on it too, the best sort of houses, luxury style.'

'Like at Claire Vista,' said Makere. Billy jumped out of his chair and his eyes jumped out, 'Brilliant, Ma, brilliant.' He planted a kiss on her unimpressed cheek and went scrabbling in a drawer for pen and paper so that he could write to Hiko:

'. . . the obvious place for the first settlement of Ngati Kangaru, it being "commodious and attractive". But more importantly, as you know, Claire Vista is the old stamping ground of our iwi that was confiscated at the end of last century, and is now a luxury holiday resort. Couldn't be apter. We must time the arrival of our people for late autumn when the holidaymakers have all left. I'll take a trip up there on Saturday and get a few snaps, which I'll send. Then I'll draw up a plan and we can do our purchases. Between us we should be able to see everyone home and housed by June next year. Timing your arrival will be vital. I suggest you book flights well in advance so that you all arrive at once. We will charter buses to take you to your destination and when you arrive we will hold the official welcome-home ceremony and see you all settled into your new homes.'

The next weekend he packed the company photographer with her camera and the company secretary with his notebook and biro, into the car. He, the company manager, got in behind the wheel and they set out for Claire Vista.

At the top of the last rise, before going down into Claire Vista, Billy stopped the car. While he was filling the radiator, he told Hana to take a few shots. And to Gavin he said, 'Have a good look, son, and write down what the eye can see.'

'On either side of where we're stopped,' wrote Gavin, 'there's hills and natral vejetation. There's this long road down on to this flat land that's all covered in houses and parks. There's this long, straight beach on the left side and the other side has lots of small beaches. There's this airport for lite planes and a red windsock showing hardly any wind. One little plane is just taking off. There's these boats coming and going on the water as far as the I can see, and there's these two islands, one like a sitting dog and one like a duck.'

Their next stop was at the Claire Vista Information Centre, where they picked up street maps and brochures, after which they did a systematic tour of the streets, stopping every now and again to take photographs and notes.

'So what do I do?' asked Tu, who had just been made legal adviser of the company. He was Tuakana Petera and this was his first employment.

'Get parchments ready for signing,' said Billy.

'Do you mean deeds of title?'

'That's it,' said Billy. Then to Rena, the company's new researcher, he said, 'Delve into the histories and see what you can come up with for new brochures. Start by interviewing Nanny.'

'I've got exams in two weeks I'll have you know.'

'After that will do.'

The next day Billy wrote to Hiko to say that deeds of title were being prepared and requested that each of the families send two thousand dollars for working capital. He told him that a further two thousand dollars would be required on settlement. 'For four thousand bucks you'll all get a posh house with boat, by the sea, where there are recreation parks, and amenities, anchorage and launching ramps, and a town, with good shopping, only twenty minutes away. Also it's a good place to set up businesses for those who don't want to fish all the time.

'Once the deeds of sale have been made up for each property I'll get the signatures on them and then they'll be ready. I'll also prepare a map of the places, each place to be numbered, and when all the first payments have been made you can hold a lottery where subscribers' tickets are put into "tin boxes". Then you can have ceremonies where the names and numbers will be drawn out by a "beautiful boy". This is a method that has been used very successfully in the past, according to my information.

'Tomorrow we're going out to buy Jew's harps, muskets, blankets (or such like) as exchange for those who sign the parchments.'

'You'll have a hundred families all living in one house, I suppose,' said Makere, 'because that's all you'll get with four thousand dollars a family.'

'Possess yourselves of the homes,' said Billy.

'What's that supposed to mean?'

'It's a "wasteland". They're waste homes. They're all unoccupied. Why have houses unoccupied when there are people wanting to occupy them?'

'Bullshit. Hana and Gav didn't say the houses were unoccupied.'

'That's because it's summertime. End of March everyone's gone and there are good homes going to waste. "Reclaiming and cultivating a moral wilderness" that's what we're doing, "serving to the highest degree", that's what we're on about, "according to a deliberate and methodical plan".'

'Doesn't mean you can just walk in and take over.'

'Not unless we get all the locks changed.'

By the end of summer the money was coming in and Billy had all the deeds of sale printed, ready for signing. Makere thought he was loopy thinking that all these rich wallahs would sign their holiday homes away.

NGATI KANGARU   117

'Not *them*,' Billy said. 'You don't get *them* to sign. You get other people. That's how it was done before. Give out pressies—tobacco, biscuits, pipes, that sort of thing, so that they, whoever they are, will mark the parchments.'

Makere was starting to get the hang of it, but she huffed all the same.

'Now I'm going out to get us a van,' Billy said. 'Then we'll buy the trifles. After that, tomorrow and the next day, we'll go and round up some derros to do the signing.'

It took a week to get the signatures, and during that time Billy and the kids handed out—to park benchers in ten different parts of the city—one hundred bottles of whisky, one hundred packets of hot pies and one hundred old overcoats.

'What do you want our signatures for?' they asked.

'Deeds of sale for a hundred properties up in Claire Vista,' Billy said.

'The only Claire Vistas we've got is where our bums hit the benches.'

'Well, look here.' Billy showed them the maps with the allotments marked out on them and they were interested and pleased. 'Waste homes,' Billy explained. 'All these fellas have got plenty of other houses all over the place, but they're simple people who know nothing about how to fully utilise their properties and they can "scarcely cultivate the earth". But who knows they might have a "peculiar aptitude for being improved". It's "high and holy work", this.'

'Too right. Go for it,' the geezers said. Billy and the kids did their rap for them and moved on, pleased with progress.

In fact everything went so well that there was nothing much left to do after that. When he wrote to Hiko, Billy recommended that settlement of Claire Vista be speeded up. 'We could start working on places for the next hundred families now and have all preparations done in two months. I think we should make an overall target of one hundred families catered for every two months over the next ten months. That means in March we get our first hundred families home, then another lot in May, July, September, November. By November we'll have five hundred Ngati Kangaru families, i.e., about four thousand people, settled before the holiday season. We'll bring in a few extra families from here (including ourselves) and that means that every property in Claire Vista will have new owners. If the Te Karere news crew comes over there again,' he wrote, 'make sure to tell them not to give our news to any other language. Hex Bro, let's just tap the sides of our noses with a little tip of finger. Keep it all nod nod, wink wink, for a while.'

On the fifth of November there was a big welcome-home ceremony, with speeches and food and fireworks at the Claire Vista hall, which had been renamed Te Whare Ngahau o Ngati Kangaru. At the same time Claire Vista was given back its former name of Ikanui and discussions took place regarding the renaming of streets, parks, boulevards, avenues, courts, dells and glens after its reclaimers.

By the time the former occupants began arriving in mid-December, all the signs in the old Claire Vista had been changed and the new families were established in their new homes. It was a lovely, soft and green life at that time of the year. One in which you could stand barefooted on grass or sand in your shorts and shirt and roll your eyes round. You could slide your boat down the ramp, cruise about, toss the anchor over and put your feet up, fish, pull your hat down. Whatever.

On the day that the first of the holidaymakers arrived at 6 Ara Hakena, with their bags of holiday outfits, Christmas presents, CDs, six-packs, cartons of groceries, snorkels, lilos and things, the man and woman and two sub-teenagers were met by Mere and Jim Hakena, their three children, Jim's parents and a quickly gathering crowd of neighbours.

At first, Ruby and Gregory in their cotton co-ordinates, and Alister with his school friend in their stonewash jeans, apricot and applegreen tees, and noses zinked pink and orange, thought they could've come to the wrong house, especially since its address seemed to have changed and the neighbours were different.

But how could it be the wrong house? It was the same windowy place in stained weatherboard, designed to suit its tree environment and its rocky outlook. There was the new skylit extension and glazed brick barbecue. Peach tree with a few green ones. In the drive in front of the underhouse garage they could see the spanking blue boat with *Sea Urchin* in cursive along its prow. The only difference was that the boat was hitched to a green Landcruiser instead of to a red Range Rover.

'That's our boat,' said Ruby.

'I doubt it,' said Mere and Ken together, folding their arms in unison.

'He paid good money for that,' a similarly folded-armed neighbour said. 'It wasn't much but it was good.'

Ruby and Alister didn't spend too much more time arguing. They went back to Auckland to put the matter in the pink hands of their lawyer.

It was two days later that the next holidaymakers arrived, this time at 13 Tiritiroa. After a long discussion out on the front lawn, Mai and Poto with their Dobermen and a contingent of neighbours felt a little sorry for their visitors in their singlets, baggies and jandals, and invited them in.

'You can still have your holiday, why not?' said Mai. 'There's the little flat at the back and we could let you have the dinghy. It's no trouble.'

The visitors were quick to decline the offer. They went away and came back two hours later with a policeman, who felt the heat but did the best he could, peering at the papers that Mai and Poto had produced, saying little. 'Perhaps you should come along with me and lay a formal complaint,' he suggested to the holidayers. Mai, Poto and a few of the neighbours went fishing after they'd gone.

From then on the holidaymakers kept arriving and everyone had to be alert, moving themselves from one front lawn to the next, sometimes having to break into groups so that their eye-balling skills, their skills in creative comment, could be shared around.

It was Christmas by the time the news of what was happening reached the media. The obscure local paper did a tame, muddled article on it, which was eclipsed firstly by a full page on what the mayor and councillors of the nearby town wanted for Christmas, and then by another, derived from one of the national papers, revealing New Year resolutions of fifty television personalities. After that there was the usual nationwide closedown of everything for over a month, at the end of which time no one wanted to report holiday items any more.

So it wasn't until the new residents began to be sued that there was any news. Even then the story only trickled.

It gathered some impetus, however, when the business-people from the nearby town heard what was happening and felt concerned. Here was this new population at Claire Vista, or whatchyoum'callit now, who were *permanent residents* and who were *big spenders*, and here were these fly-by-night jerk holidaymakers trying to kick them out.

Well, ever since this new lot had arrived business had boomed. The town was flourishing. The old supermarket, now that there was beginning to be competition, had taken up larger premises, lowered its prices, extended its lines and was providing trolleys, music and coffee for customers. The car sale yards had been smartened up and the office décor had become so tasteful that the salespeople had had to clean themselves up and mind their language. McDonald's had bought what was now thought of as a prime business site, where they were planning to build the biggest McDonald's in the Southern Hemisphere. A couple of empty storerooms, as well as every place that could be uncovered to show old brick, had been converted into better-than-average eating places. The town's dowdy motel, not wanting to be outdone by the several new places of accommodation being built along the main road, had become pink and upmarket, and had a new board out front offering television, video, heating swimming pool, spa, waterbeds, room service, restaurant, conference and seminar facilities.

Home appliance retailers were extending their showrooms and increasing their advertising. Home building and real estate was on an upward surge as more businesspeople began to enter town and as those already there began to want bigger, better, more suitable residences. In place of dusty, paintless shops and shoppes, there now appeared a variety of boutiques, studios, consortiums, centres, lands and worlds. When the Clip Joint opened up across the road from Lulu's Hairdressers, Lulu had her place done out in green and white and it became Upper Kut. After that hair salons grew all over town, having names such as Head Office, Headlands, Beyond the Fringe, Hairport, Hairwaves, Hedlines, Siz's, Curl Up and Dye.

So the town was growing in size, wealth and reputation. Booming. Many of the new businesspeople were from the new Ikanui, the place of abundant fish. These newcomers had brought their upmarket Aussie ideas to eating establishments, accommodation, shops, cinema, pre-loved cars, newspaper publishing, transport, imports, exports, distribution. Good on them. The businesspeople drew up a petition supporting the new residents and their fine activities, and this petition was eventually signed by everyone within a twenty-kilometre radius. This had media impact.

But that wasn't all that was going on.

Billy had found other areas suitable for purchase and settlement, and Rena had done her research into the history of these areas so that they knew which of the Ngati Kangaru had ancestral ties to those places. There were six areas in the North Island and six in the South. 'Think of what it does to the voting power,' said Hiko, who was on the rise in local politics. Easy street, since all he needed was numbers.

Makere, who had lost her reluctance and become wholehearted, had taken Hiko's place in the company as liaison manager. This meant that she became the runner between Ozland and Aotearoa, conducting rallies, recruiting families, co-ordinating departures and arrivals. She enjoyed the work.

One day when Makere was filling in time in downtown Auckland before going to the airport, she noticed how much of the central city had closed up, gone to sleep.

'What it needs is people,' she said to the rest of the family when she arrived home.

They were lounging, steaming themselves, showering, hairdressing, plucking eyebrows, in their enormous bathroom. She let herself down into the jacuzzi.

'Five hundred families to liven up the central city again. Signatures on papers, and then we turn those unwanted, wasteland wilderness of warehouses and office spaces into town houses, penthouses and apartments.' She lay back and closed her eyes. She could see the crowds once again seething in Queen Street renamed Ara Makere, buying, selling, eating, drinking, talking, laughing, yelling, singing, going to shows. But not only in Queen Street. Not only in Auckland. Oh, it truly was high and holy work. This Kamupene o te Hokinga Mai was 'a great and unwonted blessing'. Mind-blowing. She sat up.

'And businesses. So we'll have to line up all our architects, designers, builders, plumbers, electricians, consultants, programmers,' she said.

' "Soap boilers, tinkers and a maker of dolls' eyes" ', said Billy.

'The ones already here as well the ones still in Oz,' Makere said. 'Set them to work and use some of this damn money getting those places done up. Open up a whole lot of shops, restaurants, agencies . . . ' She lay back again with her feet elevated. They swam in the spinning water like macabre fish.

'It's brilliant, Ma,' Billy said, stripping off and walking across the floor with his toes turned up and his insteps arched—in fact, allowing only part of each heel and the ball joints of his big toes to touch the cold tile floor. With the stress of getting across the room on no more than heel and bone, his jaw, shoulders, elbows and knees became locked and he had a clench in each hand as well as in the bulge of his stomach.

'Those plumbers that you're talking about can come and run a few hot pipes under the floor here. Whoever built this place should've thought of that. But of course they were all summer people, so how would they know?' He lowered himself into the water, unlocking and letting out a slow, growling breath.

'We'll need different bits of paper for downtown business properties,' said Tu from the steam bench.

'Central Auckland was originally Ngati Whatua I suppose,' said Rena, who lost concentration on what she was doing for a moment and plucked out a complete eyebrow. 'I'll check it through then arrange a hui with them.'

'Think of it, we can influx any time of the year,' said Billy. 'We can work on getting people into the city in our off-season. January . . . And it's not only Auckland, it's every city.'

'And as well as the business places there are so many houses in the cities empty at that time of the year too,' said Makere, narrowing her eyes while Billy's eyes widened. 'So we can look at those leaving to go on holiday as well as those leaving holiday places after the season is over. We can keep on influxing from Oz of course, but there are plenty of locals without good housing. We can round them all up—the solos, the UBs, pensioners, low-income earners, street kids, derros.'

'Different papers again for suburban homes,' said Tu.

'Candidates and more candidates, votes and more votes,' said Hiko, who had come from next door wearing a towel and carrying a briefcase. 'And why stop at Oz? We've got Maori communities in Utah, in London, all over the place.'

'When do we go out snooping, Dad?' asked Hana and Gavin, who had been blow-waving each other's hair.

'Fact finding, fact finding,' said Billy. 'We might need three or four teams, I'll round up a few for training.'

'I need a video camera,' said Hana.
'Video for Hana,' said Billy.
'Motorbike,' said Gavin.
'Motorbike,' said Billy.
'Motorbike,' said Hana.
'Two motorbikes,' said Billy.
'Bigger offices, more staff,' said Tu and Rena.
'See to it,' said Billy.
'Settlements within the cities,' said Makere, who was still with solos, UB, check-out operators and such. 'Around churches. Churches, sitting there idle—wastelands, wildernesses of churches.'
'And "really of no value",' said Billy. 'Until they become . . . '
'Meeting houses,' Makere said. 'Wharenui.'
'Great. Redo the fronts, change the décor and we have all these new wharenui, one every block or so. Take over surrounding properties for kohanga, kura kaupapa, kaumatua housing, health and rehab centres, radio stations, TV channels . . .'
'Deeds of sale for church properties,' said Tu.
'More party candidates as well,' Hiko said. 'We'll need everything in place before the new coalition government comes in . . . '
'And by then we'll have "friends in high places".'
'Have our person at the top, our little surprise . . .'
'Who will be advised that it is better to reach a final and satisfactory conclusion than . . .'
' ". . . to reopen questions of strict right, or carry on an unprofitable controversy".'
'Then there's golf clubs,' said Makere.
'I'll find out how many people per week, per acre use golf courses,' said Rena. 'We'll find wasteland and wilderness there for sure.'
'And find out how the land was acquired and how it can be reacquired,' said Billy.
'Remember all the land given for schools? A lot of those schools have closed now.'

'Land given for the war effort and not returned.'
'Find out who gave what and how it will be returned.'
'Railways.'
'Find out how much is owed to us from sale of railways.'
'Cemeteries.'
'Find out what we've saved the taxpayer by providing and maintaining our own cemeteries, burying our own dead. Make up claims.'

'And there are some going concerns that need new ownership too, or rather where old ownership needs re-establishing . . .'

'Sport and recreation parks . . .'

'Lake and river retreats . . .'

'Mountain resorts . . .'

Billy hoisted himself. 'Twenty or thirty teams and no time to waste.' He splatted across the tiles. 'Because "if from *delay* you allow others to do it before you—they will succeed and you will fail",' and he let out a rattle and a shuffle of a laugh that sounded like someone sweeping up smashings of glass with a noisy broom.

'Get moving,' he said.

COMMENTARY

At first, 'Ngati Kangaru' seems to be a story which uses exaggeration for the sake of humour. It comes as a shock to any reader, to discover that the outrageous resettlement scheme which a family puts into effect to provide themselves with jobs, replicates an outrageous settlement scheme put into effect by members of the Wakefield family, in New Zealand in 1839. The story proceeds from the historical fact that Edward Gibbon Wakefield studied colonisation and wrote on the subject during a three-year gaol sentence, served in Newgate prison.

'Ngati Kangaru' tells of Billy, made redundant from his job at Mitre 10. Instead of looking for work, he is 'blobbed out in front of the two-bar heater that was expensive to run', reading a history book belonging to his university-student daughter. The Māori family is under financial pressure: four children who 'ate like elephants', the younger two at high school and the eldest with a law degree but without a job as yet. Such a predicament is familiar to many New Zealanders in the 1990s.

Less familiar are the facts revealed by the history book in question. Grace's quotations are drawn from *Fatal Success* (Burns 1989), a scholarly work by historian Dr Patricia Burns, whose material springs from primary sources—original journals, letters, diaries, parliamentary reports, legal documents, judicial inquiries and the works of Edward Gibbon Wakefield.

The historical information is a revelation to Billy. He takes a lesson from colonial history and devises a modern counterpart to the tactics used by Wakefield. Burns writes that in Wellington and in the Hutt Valley in 1839, Māori from seven major settlements were dispossessed of the land on which they lived and grew their crops. Much of the land, divided into neat rectangles, was sold in London, England, to prospective settlers as acre-sized sections for one pound an acre. Sales were completed prior to any discussion or negotiation with the Māori. In 1839, an initial 990 sections were sold by the New Zealand Company, to get in ahead of a law which would permit settlers to purchase land only from the Government.

Surveyors from England arrived at Port Nicholson, Wellington, and, according to Patricia Burns, 'measured the various pa and kainga [larger and smaller settlements] as if these did not exist. The Maori were astonished and bewildered to find Pakeha tramping over their homes, gardens and cemeteries, and in places sticking pegs in the ground . . .' (Burns 1989, pp. 151–2).

A story which alludes to theft and deception on this scale could become heavy, serious. However, Grace retains a light-heartedness that makes 'Ngati Kangaru' entertaining throughout. This is achieved, in part, through the characterisation of Billy. He's a buoyant person who enjoys his reading. The Wakefields, 'crooks, liars, cheats and thieves', appeal to his imagination and his sense of humour. He shares the joke with his wife.

> 'Listen to this,' he'd say, as Makere walked in the door on feet that during the course of the day had grown and puffed out over the tops of her shoes. And he'd attempt to interest her with excerpts from what he'd read. ' "The Wakefields' plan was based on the assumption that vast areas—if possible, every acre—of New Zealand would be bought for a trifle, the real payment to the people of the land being their 'civilising' . . ." Hee hee, that's crafty. They called it "high and holy work".'

Billy forms 'Te Kamupene o Te Hokinga Mai', meaning the 'The Company for the Return Home', for the purpose of resettling, in Aotearoa, Māori who have been living in Australia. He plans to make so-called 'waste homes' available to them for a mere $4000, that is, the holiday homes of the wealthy, at the beaches or the lakeside resorts left vacant when summer is over; just as Wakefield had described as 'wasteland' the land which provided Māori with their sustenance, that is, the land planted annually in crops like kūmara, or land covered in native bush which provided berries, roots and medicines.

Discussion Topics

1 Look at Billy's choice of language. List any words that contribute to the comical light-heartedness.

2 What is the effect of the rap, or chanted verses?

3 Explain the concept of 'waste homes'.

4 Why does Billy insist that the first group of Māori from Australia should come in autumn?

5 'Lying, cheating and stealing' are described as 'funnier' in Billy's opinion than abducting an heiress. Can you explain his attitude?

Billy's plan involves drawing up 'deeds of title'. He then intends to buy various gifts 'as exchange for those who sign the parchments.' The owners will not be the ones to sign away the properties. Instead, 'park-benchers' are glad to oblige, in exchange for a bottle of whisky. Preposterous and laughable as it may seem, it was Wakefield's tactic precisely. He gained 'legal' title to land by persuading Māori, any Māori, to provide their signatures, accepting in exchange various gifts, with no understanding of the use to be made of their signatures. At a later stage, Māori with a grudge against a neighbouring pā or leader happily signed away a neighbour's land. This approach is parodied in Billy's explanation to the 'derros' (homeless people).

'What do you want our signatures for?' they asked.
'Deeds of sale for a hundred properties up in Claire Vista,' Billy said.
'The only Claire Vista we've got is where our bums hit the benches.'

Billy then shows the map, and the location of the waste homes.

'All these fellas have got plenty of other houses all over the place, but they're simple people who know nothing about how to fully utilise their properties and they can "scarcely cultivate the earth".'

This is the very reasoning employed by Wakefield. It is doubly ironic. Whereas the Māori were highly skilled cultivators and gardeners, the holiday-makers of Claire Vista have adopted a lifestyle in which cultivation would play no part at all. The assessment of Wakefield was quite wrong and the assessment of Billy is quite right! This makes Billy's rationale even more comical—and the historical facts even more shocking. Billy's plan to bring in one hundred families every two months corresponds to the Wakefield scheme, as does his lottery system for distributing the properties among the newcomers.

Discussion Topic

What makes the story's astonishing developments credible?

Humour is sustained by Grace's attention to detail. When the holiday-makers who were the original house owners arrive at 6 Ara Hakena (the street's new name), they are described in terms of clothing which accords with the latest fashion: 'At first Ruby and Gregory in their cotton co-ordinates, and Alistair with his school friend in their stonewash jeans, apricot and applegreen tees, and noses zinked pink and orange . . .' The long list of goods carried by the holiday-makers, and the nature of the Claire Vista properties with their barbecues, boats and ramps is in stark contrast to the financial situation of Billy and his family at the story's opening.

In a story full of surprises, Grace chooses a direction which few readers could have anticipated.

Writing Or Role-play

1 After the arrival of property owners like Ruby and Gregory, what outcome did you expect?

2 Use your imagination to write an episode from the point of view of a pākehā home owner (or the son or daughter) who arrives to find the family bach occupied.
3 Role-play the above episode, involving as many of the original bach-owning family and new occupants as you wish.
4 Write your own sequel to 'Ngati Kangaru'.

'Ngati Kangaru' highlights the ongoing dispute over Māori land rights, making it a highly political short story. Revisionist historians have shown that Māori were dispossessed of many hectares of land through theft and trickery. Grace's story is satire, a literary art which invites criticism of social or political conditions existing outside the fiction. Satires usually cause us to laugh until we begin to think about the implications of the problem. Grace is highlighting the behaviour of the early colonists by applying the strategies of 1839 and 1840 to a contemporary situation. We can judge them by our present-day standards of what is fair and honest. Indirectly, Patricia Grace is justifying contemporary Māori land claims. She challenges those critical of the Māori position to re-examine our history.

Language

Readers will have found that Billy's quotations from Wakefield are the words most often used ironically, revealing the way in which language can deceive. By placing Wakefield's quotations in new contexts, Billy is able to ridicule Wakefield's business ethics and expose his total lack of understanding of Māori culture. The situation as a whole satirises the behaviour of the colonisers.

Further Discussion

1 Describe the comical situations that you enjoyed most in the story. Explain the way in which they were unexpected or exaggerated or both.

2 'Ngati Kangaru' involves social criticism. To do this, Grace uses 'irony' in which the real (underlying) meaning is the very opposite of the obvious meaning. Can you find examples of irony? What issues does the irony encourage you to think about?

3 Once she joined the family business, what improvements to her lifestyle did Makere enjoy?

4 Describe the lifestyle of Billy and his family as suggested in the last quarter of the story?' Why should Grace depict the family in this way? What observations regarding human nature does this invite?

5 Which values seem to govern contemporary life in New Zealand? What principles guided the reaction of the authorities to the events at Claire Vista, for instance?

6 Why do the centres of some cities 'close up'? Are you familiar with a large city in which there has been a clear need for urban renewal and revitalisation of the city's centre? Discuss ways in which this problem may be addressed.

GLOSSARY AND NOTES

adopt-a-chief-scheme   Edward Gibbon Wakefield proposed in a 1837 publication, *The British Colonisation of New Zealand,* that land: 'be held in reserve for chiefs until they had "learned to estimate its value". English families would "adopt" a chief, whom they would instruct and correct. He might be encouraged by "some of the more ancient and romantic institutions of the feudal age", including heraldry, with the host family conferring on the Maori "a coat of arms, somewhat similar to their own" '(Burns 1989, p.53)

Aotearoa (M)	New Zealand
baggies	fashionable baggy shorts
boulevards, avenues, courts, dells and glens	favourite words to replace 'street' in expensive suburbs
Bro	brother; but applied more broadly to friends
bullshit	nonsense
cough up	pay money
crookery	criminal practices
cuzzies	cousins
dead fireplace	no fire, probably because the family could not afford fuel
dial-a-kaumātua (M)	kaumātua means senior man or woman. The expression alludes to the 'help-lines' available to people; where you can phone for a wide range of services
derros	derelict people: homeless people, often alcoholics
eye-balling skills	traditionally, to look directly at those with whom they have a problem or with whom they are in conflict
filling the radiator	the implication is that the car is very old, since the radiator boils dry if the car climbs a hill
fly-by-night	unreliable
geezers	old people
get the hang of it	understand it
gog	look
Good on them	expression of encouragement
Goodby-ee, don't cry-ee	a typical children's taunt, when one has tricked another and thereby scored extra possessions. These words come from a popular war-time song

had a grip on it	wouldn't let it go
had the edge on	was more knowledgeable than
the Hakena family	note that this family includes three generations—three children, parents and grandparents, typical of a Māori family group
havintcha?	haven't you? Spelling reflects casual pronunciation and contributes to the mocking tone of the paragraph
he felt inspired	an ironical remark concealing anger. Those cheated by the Wakefields were the Māori. The remark also mocks a contemporary fascination with criminals, as evidenced by the proliferation of television programmes in which they feature
huffed	a sound made to express disbelief
'if from *delay* you allow others to do it before you—they will succeed and you will fail' (Burns 1989, p.14)	all quotations in 'Ngati Kangaru' can be traced to documented accounts of the policies of Wakefield and the New Zealand Company
in the clink	in prison
iwi (M)	tribal groups
jacuzzi	expensive brand of spa pool
Jeepers	exclamation of surprise
jerk holiday-makers	irresponsible, arrogant holidaymakers
kaumātua (M) housing	housing for elderly people
keep it all nod nod, wink wink	keep the plans secret. In particular, don't let the press find out
kōhanga [reo] (M)	pre-schools that provide early childhood education based on immersion in Māori language and culture

kura kaupapa (M)	Māori primary schools that teach Māori language and adopt a curriculum based on Māori values
laughing his head off	laughing heartily
lines	products
loopy	stupid
made it big	been successful
mark the parchments	sign the deeds of title (suggests the way the Māori might have have been spoken to last century when title deeds were printed on parchment)
mind-blowing	overwhelming
Mitre 10	chain of hardware stores
Nanny	name given to a Māori grandparent, male or female
New World	supermarket chain
Ngāti Whātua (M)	Māori tribe. Auckland was built on what was once their land
old stamping ground	land which the family once owned, presumably before it passed into pākehā ownership
on the bones of their arses	almost destitute
on the rise	becoming known
Orl yew need is a werthy caws.	deliberate mis-spelling to ensure that the words are read slowly and mockingly (all you need is a worthy cause)
Oz, Ozland	Australia
parchments	old-fashioned name for documents of importance
park benchers	homeless people who sleep on park benches
'Possess yourself of the soil and you are secure.'	this maxim represents Edward Gibbon Wakefield's stated philosophy (Burns 1989, p.14)

pre-loved cars	second hand cars
pressies	presents
rap	a chant, performed with rhythmical movements
recently qualified as a lawyer but was out of work	in the 1990s, it may take some time for a newly qualified person to find employment
rehab centres	rehabilitation centres (for drug addicts, etc)
rellies	relations
'scarcely cultivate the earth'; with a 'peculiar aptitude for being improved'	these quotations are from an 1837 publication written by Edward Gibbon Wakefield expressing his beliefs about the Māori people and justifying his settlement strategies (Burns 1989, p.52)
shoppes	trendy spelling of 'shops' for effect
six-packs	sets of six beer cans or bottles
snaps	photographs
solos	single parents
the story only trickled	the story came through slowly
Te Kamupene o Te Hokinga Mai (M)	the Company for the Return Home
trifles	inexpensive gifts
UBs	people on the unemployment benefit
uncle	elsewhere described as the father's cousin. Any male relative of about the father's age would be regarded as an uncle in a Māori community

these Wakefields	Edward Gibbon Wakefield organised the NZ Company settlement in Wellington in 1839. The first settlers sailed under the leadership of his brother William Wakefield, principal agent for the NZ Company. Another brother, Arthur Wakefield, became the NZ Company's agent for the Nelson settlement. Edward Jerningham Wakefield, son of Edward Gibbon, was involved in the Wanganui settlement
wallahs	people
wharenui (M)	meeting house
whatchyoum'callit	what-you-may-call-it (spelling reflects casual pronunciation) People can't pronounce the new Māori name, so they use 'whatchyoum'callit' instead

PATRICIA GRACE AND THE SHORT STORY

Since the theory of the genre was first defined by Edgar Allan Poe, it has been generally acknowledged that a short story will be tightly constructed to make every word and every image contribute to a single effect. Grace's stories are well focused and compact. Her retelling of the way Māui snared the sun in 'Sun's Marbles' must be the briefest account in print. In other stories, dialogues are pared back to a credibly terse exchange. The couple in 'Kahawai' communicate with minimal sentences and fragments of speech.

A short story's events may be small in compass but the finest stories are large in significance. Patricia Grace provides clear examples of this principle. 'Between Earth and Sky' enacts one such event, showing its importance to a particular mother; at the same time it endows with new significance a universal event. 'Sun's Marbles' integrates a lively retelling of several Māori myths with a clever allegory. While inviting us to relate ancient patterns to a contemporary context, the story is concerned with the ecology of the planet and the threat of a nuclear holocaust. 'Ngati Kangaru' puts an idea into practice and examines its consequences. At the same time, it exposes the effects of wealth on human behaviour, demonstrating the ease with which language can deceive speakers and listeners, and shows the way money speaks more loudly than justice. The apparent simplicity of Grace's stories is deceptive. The small example or the understated situation is concerned with values which underpin and guide the actions of individuals and entire communities.

At a literal level, readers can enjoy getting to know a range of characters—the elderly man who cannot conceive of graves being relocated *'tastefully'*; the father who thinks laterally to provide himself and his family with employment; the children who suck nasturtium flowers before writing their poems. Like the adults, the children in the stories are individuals.

Owen Marshall describes the short story as 'a wonderfully flexible yet powerful form, and there are as many types as there are good writers . . .' (Marshall 1994, p.2). Grace's contribution is not to push the parameters of the genre to the limit or to experiment in any startling way. Instead, she extends our experience, taking us to the marae, into the classroom of a country school, on board a fishing dinghy. She increases our understanding of the interwoven nature of love and hate, admiration and scorn, ambition and altruism in human behaviour. We participate in the action and interaction and we cannot avoid turning over and over in our minds the major issues which her stories hold up to the light.

OVERVIEW AND ANALYSIS OF A SHORT STORY

For those who will write accounts and evaluations of individual stories, answers to the following questions may help in discovering the human truths they hold.

Select a Story

1 What happens in the story? Keep it brief (three to five sentences).

2 Describe the mood of the opening. Which words help to establish that mood?

3 What can you discover about the main characters? Compare what you know of them halfway through with what you know of them at the end.

4 Is the focus on relationships, psychological study, interaction between people and environment? Or is plot important? Is there social criticism? Is the story exploring an idea?

5 Which actions and reactions carry and reveal the ideas which make the story memorable or thought provoking?

6 What is the mood of the conclusion? Show how the contrast or similarity between the moods of the opening and concluding paragraphs can contribute to the story's main focus.

7 Select a significant paragraph and say why it is effective. Consider images and imagery, sentence length and patterning, use of the unexpected and sound quality of the words chosen.

8 To what extent is your response as reader important in completing the work of the short story writer? For example, is the reader

called upon to put together ideas, to complete dialogues, to solve riddles or to question the motivation of members of a community?

9. What is the story's wider significance? What issues of universal importance are raised by the story's particular example?

BIOGRAPHICAL OUTLINE

1937	Patricia Frances Gunson was born in Wellington of Ngati Rāukawa, Ngāti Toa, Te Ātiawa descent.
1942–49	Green Street Convent, Wellington.
1950–54	St Mary's College, Wellington.
1955–56	Wellington Teacher's College.
1957	Married Kerehi Waiariki Grace of Ngāti Porou descent.
1957–85	Teacher at primary and secondary schools in King Country, Northland, Porirua. Mother of 7 children.
1976	Hubert Church Award
1982	Children's Picture Book of the Year Award
1985	Victoria University Writing Fellowship
1986	Wattie Award
1987	New Zealand Fiction Award
1988/1990	Scholarship in Letters
1989	Honorary Doctorate in Literature

PUBLICATIONS

SHORT STORIES

1975 'Waiariki'
1980 'The Dream Sleepers'
1987 'Electric City and Other Stories'
1991 'Selected Stories'
1994 'The Sky People'
1995 'Collected Stories'

NOVELS

1978 *Mutuwhenua: The Moon Sleeps*
1986 *Potiki*
1992 *Cousins*

MYTHOLOGY

1984 *Wahine Toa: Women of Maori Myth*, paintings by Robyn Kahukiwa

FOR CHILDREN

1981 *The Kuia and the Spider*
1984 *Watercress Tuna and the Children of Champion Street*
1985 Four Māori language readers for children:
He aha te mea nui?
Mā wai?
Ko au tenei
Ahakoa he iti
1993 *The Trolley*
1994 *Areta and the Kahawai*
1997 *Kei te Reti Reti Au*

BIBLIOGRAPHY

PRIMARY TEXTS

Alpers, Antony. *Maori Myths and Tribal Legends Retold by Antony Alpers*, Longman Paul, Auckland, 1964.
Grace, Patricia. *Cousins*, Penguin Books, Auckland, 1992.
——*The Dream Sleepers*, Longman Paul, Auckland, 1980.
——*Electric City and Other Stories*, Penguin Books, Auckland, 1987.
——*Mutuwhenua: The Moon Sleeps*, Longman Paul, Auckland, 1978.
——*Potiki*, Penguin Books, Auckland, 1986.
——*The Sky People*, Penguin Books, Auckland, 1994.
——*Waiariki*, Longman Paul, Auckland, 1975.
Ihimaera, Witi. 'The Seahorse and the Reef' in *The New Net Goes Fishing*, Heinemann, Auckland, 1977, pp.184–189.
Kahukiwa, Robyn & Grace, Patricia. *Wahine Toa: Women of Maori Myth*, Viking Pacific, Auckland, 1984.
Mataira, Katarina. *Maori Legends for Young New Zealanders*, Paul Hamlyn, Auckland, 1975.

SECONDARY TEXTS

Beatson, Peter. *The Healing Tongue: Themes in Contemporary Maori Literature*, Massey University, Palmerston North, 1989.
Burns, Patricia. *Fatal Success*, Heinemann Reed, Auckland, 1989.
King, Michael (ed). *Te Ao Hurihuri: The World Moves On*, Longman Paul, Auckland, 1975.
——*Tihe Mauriora: Aspects of Maoritanga*, Methuen, Wellington, 1978.
Lee, Jenny. *Notes on Patricia Grace's 'Potiki'*, Kaiako Publications, Christchurch, 1990.
Marshall, Owen (ed). *Burning Boats: Seventeen New Zealand Short Stories*, Longman Paul, Auckland, 1994.

McGregor, Graham & Williams, Mark. *Dirty Silence: Aspects of Language and Literature in New Zealand*, Oxford University Press, Auckland, 1991.

Orbell, Margaret. *Māori Myth and Legend: The Illustrated Encyclopaedia*, Canterbury University Press, Christchurch, 1995.

——*The Natural World of the Maori*, Sheridan House, New York, 1985.

Patterson, John. *Exploring Maori Values*, The Dunmore Press, Palmerston North, 1992.

Schwimmer, Eric. *The World of the Maori*, A H & A W Reed, Wellington, 1966.

ESSAYS AND ARTICLES

Bardolph, Jacqueline. ' "A Way of Talking": A Way of Seeing: The Short Stories of Patricia Grace', *Commonwealth: Essays and Studies*, vol. 12, no. 2, 1990, pp.23–39.

Corballis, Richard. 'Patricia Grace', *The Reference Guide to Short Fiction*, Noelle Watson (ed), St James Press, Detroit, 1994, pp.217–218.

Cox, Nigel. 'Living in Both Worlds', *Quote Unquote*, vol. 12, 1994, p.9.

McCrae, Jane. 'Patricia Grace—Interviewed by Jane McCrae', *In the Same Room: Conversations with New Zealand Writers*, Elizabeth Alley & Mark Williams (eds), Auckland University Press, Auckland, 1992, pp.284–296.

——'Patricia Grace and Complete Communication', *Australian and New Zealand Studies in Canada*, vol. 10, 1993, pp.66–86.

Pearson, Bill. 'Witi Ihimaera and Patricia Grace', *Critical Essays on the New Zealand Short Story*, Cherry Hankin (ed), Heinemann, Auckland, 1982, pp.166–183.

Robinson, Roger. ' "The Strands of Life and Self": The Oral Prose of Patricia Grace', *CRNLE Reviews Journal*, vol. 1, 1993, pp.13–27.

Simms, Norman. 'A Maori Literature in English: Prose Fiction—Patricia Grace', *Pacific Moana Quarterly*, vol. 3, no. 2, 1978, pp.186–199.

Tausky, Thomas. ' "Stories That Show Them Who They Are": An Interview with Patricia Grace', *Australian and New Zealand Studies in Canada*, vol. 6, 1991, pp.90–102.

Wevers, Lydia. 'Short Fiction by Maori Writers', *Commonwealth: Essays and Studies*, vol. 16, no. 2, 1994, pp.26–33.